MW01138219

Apples
Should Be
Red

A ROMANTIC COMEDY NOVELLA

PENNY WATSON

APPLES SHOULD BE RED

Copyright © 2014 Nina Roth Borromeo

Cover Design: Penny Reid
Cover Images: iStock (Alexandra Draghici)
Editorial: Helen Hardt
Formatting: Stone Lily Design

All rights reserved. Except for the use in any review, the reproduction or utilization of this work in whole or in any form by any electronic, mechanical or other means is forbidden without the express permission of the author.

This is a work of fiction. Names, characters, places and incidents are either the product of the author's imagination or are used fictitiously, and any resemblance to actual persons, living or dead, business establishments, events or locales is entirely coincidental.

Acknowledgments

Huge thanks to the Junior Mints for support, encouragement, and friendship.

Thanks to my readers, blogger pals, and colleagues, who put up with my quirks and antics.

Special thanks to Julia Barrett, and my non-romance reading friends Jill and Sarah, who give me perspective from the other side of the fence.

ONE

THE KIDS

"**I would like** to reiterate that I think this is a horrible idea. Awful. What the hell were we thinking?" Karen let out a long-suffering sigh and glared at her husband.

John attempted to toss his empty beer bottle into the recycling bin. He missed. It rolled across the warped kitchen floor and stopped a couple of inches from the door.

"You're overreacting. It's not that big a deal. Your mom can handle my dad for a few days. We'll be there Thursday. How bad could it be?"

Karen leaned over to collect the errant bottle. She whipped it side arm across the kitchen. It sailed right under the counter and banked off the back of the bin. John was impressed. But then again, she often impressed him. The woman could cook like a pro, throw a perfect spiral football, and blow him till his eyes crossed. She

APPLES SHOULD BE RED

was a great wife. But she worried about her mom. And although he wouldn't admit it, she might have a good reason to at the moment.

"Your dad is a son-of-a-bitch. He has no social skills, hates visitors, and is down-right combative when anyone tries to tell him what to do." She planted a hand on her denim-covered hip and took a deep breath. Her breasts, plump and ripe, rose and fell under John's watchful eyes. "My mom is polite to a fault, wants to please everyone, and gives advice like Dear Freakin' Abby. Those two are going to kill each other after spending three days together. I should have booked a room for my mom at the South Hardin Inn."

John pushed himself off the island and sauntered over to Karen. He planted his arms on either side of her lush hips and smiled. "Honey. We tried to get her a room. It was booked because of the holiday. There's nothing we can do. Your mom and my dad will manage to survive three days alone together, and everything will be fine." Secretly, he was thinking Mrs. Anderson might end up sleeping in her car after twenty-four hours. Maybe twelve. His dad was tough. John shrugged and lowered his face to his wife's cleavage. "Nice view."

Karen giggled. "Don't try to distract me, you horn dog."

He rubbed his face back and forth and then howled mournfully.

Karen grabbed a handful of his hair and yanked

up his head.

"Ow! Take it easy, hon." Well, hell. She had that goofy look in her eye. They could probably squeeze in a quick BJ before the game started.

"I can't believe we got a burst pipe this week. Thank God Joey can repair it tomorrow. Hopefully my mom will make the best of it." She kissed his forehead. It was sappy, but he loved it when she did that. "I guess my mom will stay busy cooking Thanksgiving dinner. We'll probably have a seventy-two course meal by the time we get there."

He laughed. "Yeah. With my dad's head on a platter."

Karen laughed, too. "With an apple stuffed in his mouth."

"And a cigarette hanging out the side."

"My mom makes really good apple stuffing." Karen bit her lip. She was still nervous, he could tell. He slid down to the floor and kissed the front of her jeans.

"How 'bout I stuff you, sweet thing?"

Karen shook her head. "You have a way with words, John."

He missed half of the first quarter.

THE OLD COOT

"Frank Bucknell is a fucking retard." Tom took a long, lingering drag on his cigarette and squinted at the checkout girl. "There is no way in hell that grill is worth more than three hundred. Seven hundred for a grill? Bullshit."

The checkout girl sent him a glazed look. "Whatevs. We don't allow smoking in here, Mr. Jenkins. And the grill is six hundred and ninety nine dollars. Plus tax. Do you want one?"

He ashed on the floor. "Not for seven hundred goddamned dollars I don't. I'll head over to Evanston and see if I can get a better deal there."

The girl shrugged.

"What the fuck does 'whatevs' mean? Is that some sort of code for 'I'm too fucking lazy to speak English?'"

"Yeah. That's it." Little Miss Attitude rolled her eyes at him. Rolled her fucking eyes! The girl would probably get pregnant, drop out of high school, and mooch off his motherfucking taxes for the rest of her life. Jesus.

Tom dropped his cigarette on the dirty wood floor of Bucknell's Hardware and ground it out with the heel of his boot.

"That's a fire hazard, Mr. Jenkins." The checkout girl was getting cocky.

"Huh. A fire is probably Bucknell's secret desire. Insurance money and a one-way ticket to Seaside, Florida." He hacked up a gruff laugh and sighed. Now he had to drive all the way to Evanston, goddammit.

This whole holiday bullshit was going to drive him to drink.

More.

Drink more.

Thanksgiving was always a pain in the ass. He dragged himself to John's house for the fake "family time" thing because his daughter-in-law insisted. He was sure John would be perfectly happy to get take-out from the grocery store and watch football with a six-pack. Or two.

But no.

Miss Fancy Pants Karen had to host a traditional Thanksgiving meal. With real china, silver, and a dried-out turkey that not even a gallon of gravy could save. She and her mom were two birds-of-a-feather.

But this year fate had tossed a giant wrench into the holiday plans. John and Karen's house was under renovation, and Karen's mom had a termite infestation that involved a five-day tent job. They'd asked Tom to host. He figured what the hell, he'd throw a bird on his grill with a beer in its ass and slide a can of cranberry onto a plate. Mrs. Anderson, Karen's mom, would be horrified. Which made the whole debacle even more appealing. She was so buttoned-up, he wondered how she didn't choke on her perfect strand of pearls. Four, maybe five hours of entertaining. Not so bad. And the ladies would clean up the colossal mess he was sure to make in the kitchen.

But then a pipe burst at John's place, and Mrs. Anderson needed somewhere to crash. And John and Karen wouldn't be arriving until the plumbing was fixed.

Beverly was on her way.

Fuck.

He had no idea what Mrs. Beverly Anderson expected. But he wasn't a goddamned bed-and-breakfast. Also, he wasn't feeling particularly welcoming. Mrs. Anderson was a snooty-ass bitch, and her late husband, who'd keeled over from heart disease the year before, had been a slimy snake dressed up in a three-piece suit.

Tom pulled out a rumpled pack of Marlboros from his front shirt pocket and grunted. Empty.

Fuck.

MRS. ANDERSON

"What do you mean, you don't have fresh sage? It's Thanksgiving Week." Mrs. Beverly Anderson gripped the shopping cart handle so hard her knuckles turned white and started to burn. She forced herself to relax. Fingers splayed out, diamonds glinting in the fluorescent lights of Greene's Shopping Center. Straighten, bend, straighten, bend. She placed her hands lightly on the handle and tapped one perfectly rounded burgundy nail on the plastic guard.

"Of course you have sage. It's mandatory for a proper gravy and stuffing."

The employee had the decency to look sheepish. "I'm sorry, ma'am. But we ran out of sage this morning. We should have more in tomorrow."

This time Bev gripped the handle so tight, her nails dug into the soft, pink, vulnerable skin of her palms, tattooing them with crescent moons.

"I won't be here tomorrow. I need it. Now. I need it now."

The young man shook his head. "Sorry, Ma'am." He resumed the preposterous task of organizing golden apples in the bin. So they were all lined up, stems out, like a Warhol painting.

Golden apples were a complete waste of time. Not sweet enough for pies or cakes. Not crisp enough for a snack. Not red enough.

Apples should be red.

She took a deep, cleansing breath. In with the good air, out with the bad air. She'd seen this advice somewhere, a long time ago. Perhaps in a woman's magazine.

But all the air was bad. It smelled like sweaty workers, fish from the seafood section, mildew and mold, desperation. Imperfection.

Bad air.

Bev swallowed. "Well, I guess I'll just have to do a spot of shopping in Hardin. Hopefully the grocery store there will be better prepared for the holiday." She sent the young man a sullen look, but he completely ignored her.

Just like Roger used to do.

Invisible. Ignorable. Like an end table next to the sofa. No one ever notices the end table. A spot for the lamp. A place for the dusty family photo, smiles wide and frozen, too much perfume. The nineteenth century French coffee table, with inlaid edging, was the focal point of the room. Spotless, dust-free, a conversation piece. Never ignored. A mistress in a bright red sweater and red lipstick.

She released her death grip on the handle.

Straighten, bend, straighten, bend.

In a way, it was a good thing there was no sage. It would give her an excuse to shop and avoid Tom. He was a horrible, rude man. Crude and raw. She would steer clear of him as much as possible. Perhaps she could hide on the porch. His porch had a rocking chair, and as far as she could tell, it had never been used. It looked like a lovely spot to read or knit and enjoy the view.

Tom Jenkins was hardly a man to enjoy the view. He hated everyone, and everything. And talked about it all the time.

Bev wasn't feeling very thankful this November.

She ripped a bag off the rack and began to place Red Cortland apples inside.

Two

Gentlemen, Take
Your Corners

Beverly parked the BMW in front of Tom's house. It was clear as day this was a bachelor's residence. Clumps of tall grass skirted the porch, and dandelions dotted the front lawn. It always baffled her that the front of his home—the most important part of the house, the side the neighbors would see, and judge, and discuss—was disorganized and drab. But the back yard—hidden from view, and worthless since Tom never entertained—was perfectly maintained. He had a fifty square foot vegetable garden in the back that he coddled like a fussy baby.

Bev shook her head as she surveyed the mess. She wouldn't trade her immaculate colonial for this disaster in a million years. But she did covet that porch. A colonial did not invite lingering. You entered the house, conducted your business, went about your day. The farmer's porch was an invitation to leisure. Lazing about on an Adirondack chair, sipping tart lemonade from a sweaty glass, dawdling. There had been very little dawdling at her residence, 189 Beddington Lane. And now, a widow at the age of fifty-nine, Bev didn't have the slightest idea how to dawdle. Thirty-seven years of servitude to her late husband had guaranteed that.

She got out of the car and debated asking Tom for help. There were boxes of cooking supplies and food in the back of her vehicle, but Tom was just as likely to watch her struggle as he was to lend a hand. She could picture him leaning against the porch railing with a lit cigarette in his mouth and that smug little smirk. With his legs crossed, like he didn't have a care in the world. And her dressed in nice slacks and a cardigan and two-inch heels, carting around bags of stuffing mix and cans of broth.

Tom was an ass.

She opened the back door of the sedan and slid the cartons to the edge of the leather seat. A beat-up truck barreled down the street, sprayed gravel onto her bumper, and turned into the driveway.

Of course. Even his truck was rude.

Tom unrolled his window and leaned out to peer into her back seat. The truck idled in the driveway, muffler rattling.

"You know. We have food in Hardin. You didn't need to bring your own." He paused and lit the cigarette dangling from his lips.

"Hello Tom. It's nice to see you."

"I guess our groceries aren't hoity-toity enough for you, huh?" He squinted at her as a plume of smoke curled around his bushy eyebrows.

"Happy Thanksgiving." She hefted a box of fresh vegetables into her arms.

"For Christ's sake. I have a vegetable garden. Why did you waste your money on those?"

"Thank you so much for hosting dinner this year."

Tom spit out the window. "Hope you don't mind if we eat on paper plates."

She hesitated for just a split second and Tom smiled. She had a perverse desire to smash his face with the box she held.

"You don't mind, do you? Bev?"

"I'm sure dinner will be lovely. Please excuse me while I carry these boxes inside."

"Knock yourself out."

Bastard. They were all alike. Roger used to sit on the couch, laughing at some inane television show, while she spent all afternoon preparing his dinner.

And he never, not once, not once in thirty-seven years, ever said thank you.

Paper plates.

Over my dead body.

Beverly Anderson had commandeered his kitchen. She had bottles of wine lined up next to his toaster. Crates of vegetables stacked on the table. Bunches of herbs already cut and placed in glasses of water, sucking up the fluoride from his tap. Her lips were pursed. She had some god-awful flesh-colored lip gloss on. It reminded him of a slimy piece of smoked salmon. Jesus. Those shiny lips were pursed and judgmental and clearly finding fault with his perfectly reasonable kitchen.

What a bitch.

"Bev, you whipping up something for lunch?"

She didn't even glance his way. "No. I need to reorganize. To prepare for Thanksgiving dinner."

"Thanksgiving is three days from now. Are you going to eat anything between now and then?"

"Of course. But first things first."

"How about first things second and lunch first?"

She reached overhead to grab something from a cabinet, and Tom watched her silky little cardigan ride up. Her ass still looked pretty good for her age. He wondered what she would do if he gave her a good hard slap.

She turned to him and narrowed her eyes. "Why are you smiling at me?"

He grunted. "No reason. So what's for lunch?"

Bev folded her arms across her chest and the bangles on her wrists jangled. "What do you normally eat for lunch?"

"I like tuna melts. I like egg salad. I like roast beef sandwiches with horseradish. I like burgers with mayo."

"Do you cook these items yourself?" she asked

innocently.

Too late, Tom saw the trap. "Um." He cleared his throat. "I do. But they always taste better when someone else makes them." He shot her a smile, pretty much resigned to her dinging him anyway.

Unexpectedly, Bev laughed.

He quirked a brow. He was used to hearing her strained chuckle. But he had never heard the real thing. A real honest-to-God laugh.

"You have a lot of chutzpah, Mr. Jenkins. Has anyone ever told you that?"

"As a matter fact, I hear that a lot."

She smiled.

He really wanted to wipe off that god-awful lip gloss.

"I am not in the least bit surprised to hear that." She turned back to the cabinets and sighed. "Has it ever occurred to you to organize the canned goods, spices, and sauces into different areas? By alphabetical order? So you can find things efficiently? It would certainly make life easier."

"No." His stomach growled.

"No? How do you find anything in here?"

He shrugged. "I rummage around until I find it. And if I can't find, I go buy a new one."

Beverly slid several cans to the left of the cabinet. "Let's start here. A for artichokes."

"A for artichokes. That sounds like a children's book. That a hippy farmer would write." His stomach growled again. "So how about lunch?"

"You are nothing if not stubborn."

"You have no idea."

"I have a very good idea, actually. Do you have eggs?"

"Yes, I have eggs." He tried not to gloat. She was going to make lunch!

"I suppose I could take a few minutes to prepare egg salad. I have celery, chives, and onions for my stuffing. I could spare a bit for some egg salad."

"Oh no. I don't like that shit in my egg salad. Just eggs and mayo. Maybe some salt and pepper."

Beverly hooked one perfectly manicured finger through her pearls and wrinkled her brow. "The word 'salad' implies additions to the mixture. Vegetables and herbs. Celery, onions, perhaps scallions, even sweet pepper. And I usually add dill, but we could use parsley instead…"

"No. I hate that crap. Why do you have to go and spoil a good thing? Egg salad should be eggs and mayo. The end."

"Mr. Jenkins, if you would like me to prepare egg salad for you, I will do it my way. The right way. If you don't approve, then maybe you should prepare your own lunch."

Goddammit! He contemplated picking out all the shit from the egg salad for a couple of seconds. Then decided the hell with it.

"Forget it. I'm going to the diner." He glared at her, waiting for her to back down. Waiting for her to accommodate him.

Waiting.

She tilted up her chin, just a bit. Enough for him to know she was digging in her heels.

"Have a nice meal at the diner, Mr. Jenkins."

He grabbed his truck keys and slammed the door on the way out.

A is for artichokes.

Jesus H. Christ!

Three

Stepping In Chicken Shit

Beverly peered over the edge of the fence in the backyard. Unlike the charming vegetable gardens she saw in glossy magazines, which were always enclosed by a white picket fence and had lush morning glory vines rambling up the stumps, Tom's garden looked like something out of a prison. There was wavy chicken wire strung between recycled posts. Jagged sticks topped the railing, jutting out in a most unwelcoming manner. There were no sweet garden gnomes, or birdbaths, or crooked signs heralding "The Garden." There were no colorful flowers. No birdhouses mounted on poles. Just row after row after row of cabbage, onion stalks, broccoli. Nothing was labeled.

The smell practically knocked her off her feet. Her landscape always smelled like freshly cut grass and impatiens. This smelled horrible. Like waste and decay.

"What do you think?"

She jumped. "Please don't do that, Tom. I hate it when you sneak up on me like that." She twisted her pearls in her curled fingers.

"Why do you think I do it?" he chuckled. He nodded at the garden. "Pretty goddamned impressive, isn't it?"

Bev suppressed the urge to roll her eyes. He was puffing up with pride, like a strutting rooster.

"I suppose so."

"You suppose so?" Tom shouted. "Have you ever grown a vegetable garden? *Bev?*"

She hated the tone he used when saying her name. Roger used to do that. An inflection insinuating she was an idiot. The image of her stabbing Tom with a pitchfork popped into her head.

She took a deep breath. "No, I have not. I concentrate on perennials, annuals, and shrubs."

"Nonessentials." He glared at her.

"I'm not sure I'm following your train of thought."

"You know exactly what I'm saying, you uptight—" He stopped, pulled out a fresh package of cigarettes from his shirt pocket and pounded the pack on his palm. "You're all about form, not function, Bev. Your garden looks pretty, but it doesn't *do* anything. Your house looks pretty, but nothing ever gets accomplished there. *You* look pretty, but…"

Her teeth were snapped so tightly together, she could feel the muscles in her jaw ache. "But what, Mr. Jenkins?"

"You know, you're stepping in chicken shit."

Tom whistled as he ambled away.

Bev glanced down at her feet. Manure dotted her three hundred dollar designer leather pumps.

She eyed the pitchfork leaning against the fence as she turned back to the house.

"Why are there jagged sticks at the top of the fence?"

Beverly and Tom sat across from each other at the kitchen table, eating a store-bought chicken potpie for dinner. Bev thought it was bland. Tom had smothered his in hot sauce. She stared out the window at his garden as dusk settled.

"Keep out the raccoons."

She stopped eating. "What are you talking about?"

Tom shook salt on his dinner. "I got critter problems. Gophers tunnel under the fence, raccoons climb over. I have the chicken wire buried three feet deep. Keeps the gophers and moles under control. But the god-damned raccoons are surprisingly agile. I've seen one scurry up the wooden posts. My sharp topper will pierce their eyes, their face. I didn't spend hundreds of hours of hard labor to feed those furry fuck-wads."

Bev tensed every time Tom cussed. Which was probably why he did it so frequently in her presence. Roger always said Tom was a low-life. But the truth was Tom was more educated than Roger. He just didn't care about his appearance or car or what anyone else thought. What a thorn in Roger's side. This cranky, miserable old man, who'd started his career as an engineer, educated at Caltech, now worked as a contractor. Roger, a car salesman, could never understand why a man would trade in a suit job for greasy fingernails and a power saw.

"Is there no other way to prevent the raccoons from eating your garden?" She was surprised to find she was genuinely interested in the answer.

He nodded. "Poison. Cayenne pepper. Traps. One of them impaled himself on a stick one night. I left the carcass there for a while. That did the trick."

Bev sucked in a breath. "That is sickening. Sick. You are a horrible man. You left his dead body—"

"Don't get your knickers in a bunch. They're pests. And they're a nuisance."

"I don't care. That is foul and disgusting." She shuddered and put down her fork. She'd lost her appetite.

"I'll bet if you had raccoons and gophers eating up your perfect little flower beds, you'd hire some landscaping company to come out and 'eliminate' the problem for you. How do you think they do that? Invite the little fuckers to tea and politely ask them to leave the premises? Fuck, no. They kill them. Do you know how the poison works?"

"I don't want to know." She wrapped her fingers around her pearls and peered down at her empty plate. It was paper. He had won that round.

Tom reached over and touched her collarbone. He ran his callused fingers over her skin and tapped the pearls. "I can't believe you're still wearing these."

Bev stilled like a startled wild animal. Tom continued to rub her skin. His fingertips were rough and leathery, nicotine-stained. She felt the brush of that touch all the way down to her polished toes, all the way to the top of her salon-perfect hair, to every fiery nerve in her body.

Her late husband's touch had made her cringe with nausea.

This.

This.

This was different.

"Why wouldn't I wear the pearls, Tom?" she asked. Her voice cracked.

He shrugged his shoulders and slouched back in his chair. "I'm just surprised. I thought the second old Rog keeled over, you would lighten up. Lose the tight bun, the attitude. He had you under his thumb for so long, maybe it's too late."

"Is that what you did when Alberta died?"

"No, Alberta... Well, that was different. She'd been sick for months. It was like she didn't even exist. Didn't talk. I didn't have any animosity toward her. Just felt bad at the end. For her suffering."

Bev focused on her breathing. She did not want to hyperventilate in front of this man. "And you think I had animosity toward my husband? Is that what you think? Not, I might add, that it's any of your business. And it's extremely poor manners to discuss this at the dinner table."

"You wanna talk about it on the porch?" Tom kept a straight face, but she knew he was laughing inside.

"I don't want to talk about it at all."

"Because your late husband was such a bastard? Treated you like crap for almost forty years? I'd wanna talk about it. I'd take the pearls and chuck them right into the chicken shit pile. He didn't deserve you. You should have—"

"Enough!" She was shaking. She jerked up from the table and knocked over her chair. "You." Deep breath. "You." Black stars dotted her vision. Her legs began to crumble.

She closed her eyes as Tom's arms wrapped around her. "Take a nice even breath, Bev. No use getting so worked up about the motherfucker. I'm just giving you shit." Tears leaked down the sides of her face. Tom's arms were strangely comforting. He smelled like sweat and oil. His whiskers tickled the side of her face. "Better?"

Her eyes fluttered open. "Yes. Please pardon my overreaction."

"There's nothing to be—"

"If you'll excuse me, I'd like to get ready for bed."

Tom sighed. "I'll get you some fresh sheets."

His gaze, icy blue, searched her face. She stared back, unblinking.

Fifteen minutes later she put on her nightgown.

She glanced at her reflection in the mirror over the dresser. Those fifty-one beads winked back, lustrous in the dim light. She ran her fingers over the gems. Each one soft. Luminous. Perfect.

Beverly removed the pearls and placed them in her travel case, snapping it shut in the silence.

FOUR

This was his favorite time of day. Early morning. He perched his ass on the edge of the porch steps and sipped a cup of coffee. Instant. When the kids visited, they pulled out his coffee maker and brewed up something gourmet. He knew Bev was a tea-drinker, so she wouldn't care.

He'd pushed her too far last night.

Once he'd been at a hotel job, working on a renovation project, and he'd seen Roger. Bev's late husband had reminded him of a weasel. Long narrow nose, weak chin, pasty white and pudding-soft. The woman giggling in his ear hadn't been much better. She was stuffed into a tight red dress like a slutty sausage, and her grating laugh had echoed off the walls of the lobby. Roger had lipstick stains on his shirt collar and a tent in the front of his polyester pants. Tom had made sure he wasn't seen. He had no interest in that bullshit melodrama. Hell, as far as he knew, Bev knew all about it.

If he'd had Roger as a spouse, the first thing he would have done after the douchebag croaked would be to paint the house neon fucking orange. Then he'd rip out all the perfect little flowers lined up like toy soldiers in the front yard. Sell the BMW, get a convertible. Chuck the librarian ensemble, dress in ratty jeans. Jump in the car. Live it up. Travel.

But Bev was still in that house, still immaculate as always. Same clothes, same tight bun. Same repressed personality. Just once he would like her to explode like a motherfucking volcano and cuss him out. Say something honest. He'd like to pop her like a boil and watch the bubbling pus leak out. No doubt about it, Bev was filled with pus. Roger had made sure of that.

He usually got a kick out of busting her chops. But last night…last night the look she'd given him lacked the haughty attitude she usually wrapped around her like a shield. That look was vulnerable. It made him feel sort of sick to his stomach, jabbing her when she didn't fight back.

That sure took the fun out of the game.

Tom wasn't going to deal with the inexplicable sexual chemistry that had reared up when he touched her. She was clearly as shocked as he was. He'd bet a million motherfuckin' dollars that Beverly Anderson had never had an orgasm in her life. Christ.

The porch door squeaked. "Tom?"

He turned to see Bev's shadowy figure through

the screen. "Come on out on the stoop. Get yourself a cup of tea."

"I already did." She clasped the tea like a lifeline.

"You look like a nun. Is that what nuns wear to bed?"

Bev graced him with a small smile. He noted her puffy eyes, but the smile seemed genuine.

"I don't know what nuns wear to bed, Tom. But this is a perfectly respectable bathrobe and slippers." She glanced at his ratty T-shirt and jeans. "You're one to talk about wardrobe choices."

"I'm comfortable. Got no one to impress."

She stepped onto the porch, clutching the tea so tightly he was scared she'd shatter the mug.

"Take a load off, Bev. Sit on the stoop and watch the world go by. Let's see what my neighbors are up to this morning."

She hesitated. "I'll sit on the rocker…"

"No, sit on the stoop."

"Why are you so bossy?"

"Why are you so stubborn?"

Bev barked out a laugh. "Me? Me stubborn? You are the most stubborn man I've—"

"It's not the same thing," he said. "The rocker. There's something about sitting on the stoop. It's just better. Try it."

"I'm too old. I don't think my knees can take it."

"For Christ's sake, Bev. You're not that old. Late fifties isn't old. Ninety-five is old. I'm sixty-two and still sprightly."

She refused to make eye contact with him.

"I'll help you. I promise." Tom had no freaking idea why he was so damned insistent Bev sit on the stoop, but for some reason it seemed important. He stood up and held out his hand to her. "Come on."

She stared at his hand for a good sixty seconds. Neither one of them moved. Finally she let go of the mug and reached for him.

Her hands were soft, her nails perfect. Her pale little fingers got lost inside his dark leathery mitt. He tugged. "Come on."

She pursed her lips but followed him. He led her to the third step down, and they both sat. Bev took a minute to wrap her robe securely around her. Two fuzzy slippers lined up next to each other below the hem of her pink nightgown.

"Now we watch."

Bev looked amused. "What exactly are we watching, and why do we need to do it *here* instead of on the perfectly lovely rockers that look as though they have never been used?"

He pulled out a cigarette and lit it. "The teenagers down the street have been sneaking out all the time. I'm waiting to see when the parents will catch on. If ever." He pointed his cigarette at the dingy Victorian across from him. "Mrs. Martin lives there. She's a sanctimonious prig. And she's having an affair with her Mexican gardener. Thinks no one notices, but I do." He smirked. "A couple of hippy professors live on the corner. I think they're swingers. Lots of sexy young couples coming and going. Probably smoking pot and having orgies. Got some new folks moving in next door, too. Should be interesting to see what they're up to."

"I know what you're trying to do."

"Hmm."

"It's not going to work."

"Hmm."

"You're trying to embarrass me. You love to make me uncomfortable. See if you can make me squirm. Don't you have anything better to do?"

Tom ignored her. "Look. There. Down the street. See that kid sliding down the porch roof?"

Bev rolled her eyes, but she complied. They watched the kid contemplate the best way to jump off the two-story roof onto the lawn below. Tom figured the boy was missing quite a few brain cells after smoking drugs every day after school for years.

"You don't think he's going to—"

"Jump? Yep. I think he is."

Bev looked startled. "Dear Lord! He's going to break his leg!"

"Yep. Probably will." Tom ashed on the weeds growing in front of the porch.

The boy attempted to crawl down the rickety trellis on the side of the house.

Bev started to laugh. "Oh my God. That looks like a climbing rose. It's covered with huge thorns. That boy is going to be covered with scratches."

The kid jumped. His foot got caught in the trellis,

and he took the whole thing down with him. It made an enormous crash and the idiot started screaming bloody murder.

Bev choked. "Tom. Tom. Are we going to—"

"Nope."

"But…"

"…help…"

"Nope." He turned to Bev. "You're not quite grasping this whole sitting-on-the-stoop thing. We sit. And we watch. We don't get involved."

They could hear the boy bawling down the street. What a loser.

"Oh. My. Goodness." Bev's eyes were riveted on his next door neighbor's upstairs window.

"That…that…that man…"

Tom snorted, then started to laugh. He finished off with a hacking fit. It took him a couple of moments to catch his breath.

"You're amused, Mr. Jenkins."

"I see you've discovered Mr. DiBenedetto."

"The naked man next door? Yes. You have a very colorful neighborhood."

"Everyone has a colorful neighborhood, Bev. You just gotta look for the colors."

He glanced over at her and made a decision. "Do you have any normal clothes with you?"

"Normal? All of my clothes…"

"Not fancy. Regular clothes. If you're weeding your garden at home, what do you wear?"

"I have dungarees, gardening clogs, and an old

T-shirt with an apron…"

"Do you have any of those clothes here?"

"As a matter of fact, I did bring my casual clothes. I thought I could help you in the garden." She paused. "If you wanted my help."

"I want your help."

Goddamn if her eyes didn't light right up. Chocolate brown eyes, like a motherfucking puppy dog.

He was screwed.

He stood up and offered her a helping hand. She grasped his fingers and stood, slowly. Her knees were trouble, he could tell.

"Go change into your jeans." He took a last puff on his cigarette and threw it into a clay pot filled with water next to the steps. "And cut your nails. You can't work on the garden with nails like that."

"I wear gardening gloves…"

"Nope. You can't feel the soil with gloves on. Cut your nails."

"Tom!"

"Don't fight with me, woman. And don't bother with all the makeup and perfume and that god-awful lip gloss. You'll attract every freakin' bug in the state of California. Got it?"

"You don't like my lip gloss?" Her brow furrowed.

"No. You don't need that shit. Your lips look fine just the way they are."

She was staring at him like she'd never seen him before.

"I'll meet you in the garden in fifteen minutes."

"Tom…"

"What?"

"Why do you just watch? On the stoop? Don't you ever speak to you neighbors? It seems…"

Tom raised an eyebrow. "What?" he snapped.

Bev shook her head. "Just seems antisocial. Watching and never speaking to any of them."

"Got nothing to say to them. They're busy with their lives. I'm busy with my life. Most of them are a bunch of idiots anyway."

"I remember, when Alberta was alive, you had cookouts in the backyard, and she always had that cookie exchange at Christmas—"

"Yeah, well, that was Alberta. She liked to chitchat with the neighbors and make Ritz cracker snacks. I don't do that shit."

Bev was quiet for a moment, then nodded. "I'll get changed."

Tom reached for another cigarette. So she thought he was antisocial. Well, she was right. He was antisocial. Most folks weren't worth the trouble.

He needed to take his morning dump.

And then he was going to heartily enjoy mussing up Mrs. Anderson.

Bev gingerly stepped on the edge of the garden plot, trying not to sink into a pile of fertilizer. She could just imagine the feel of chicken poop compost squishing into her gardening clogs.

She shuddered.

"Well, that's better." Tom surveyed her from head to toe and nodded approvingly. He struck a match and lit his ubiquitous cigarette. "Except for one thing." He dropped a pair of enormous boots on the ground. "Change into these. You don't want chicken shit on your feet."

"Those are too big, Tom, I'm—"

He kneeled down and grabbed her heel.

"Now just one minute. Don't even…"

Tom ripped off her garden clog and flung it across the lawn.

"Tom! Stop it."

He smiled through the cigarette as he shoved the boot onto her foot.

She was extremely uncomfortable with the idea that someone else's dirty work boot was now on her body. Filled with soil, and muck, and God-knew-what-else.

"Take this off right—"

He snatched the other clog and she almost toppled over. Bev laid a hand on top of his head to steady herself. He wore a faded baseball cap. She liked the feel of it under her fingertips.

She peered down at him. He was brown and rough all over, the exact opposite of Roger. Roger had been soft. He'd had no clue how to fix a leaky toilet or seal a deck or plant a garden. He'd spent his days at a desk and his nights in front of the television.

Or elsewhere.

Tom was lean and hard all over. His dark arms were corded with muscle, his long legs encased in Carhartts. His face always looked prickly with whiskers, something Roger would have never permitted. Her late husband had shaved religiously every day, following up with a generous dose of cologne.

The most disconcerting thing about Tom Jenkins was the feel of his gaze. Icy blue eyes, intense hot glare. Most days it made her uncomfortable, the way he looked at her.

Today wasn't so bad.

Before she realized what was happening, the other boot was jammed onto her foot. Now she looked ridiculous. In her Scripps T-shirt and dungarees and two enormous dirty boots.

Tom stood up and smiled. "Perfect fit." Then he hacked from laughing so hard. Bev felt like whacking him on the back.

He captured her hands for inspection. "Your nails are still—"

She tugged her hands away from his grasp and pulled out work gloves from her back pocket. "My nails are fine. I'm wearing gloves." She squinted at him in the bright sunshine. "Where do you want me to start? Weeding?"

Tom took a step closer to her. She smelled his detergent, his soap, tobacco, and coffee. He removed his cap by the brim and placed it gently on her head.

"It's sunny today. This will keep you from getting a burn."

His cap perched lightly on her hair, just above her ponytail. She could still feel his heat from the hat warming the top of her head. She had his cap on top, his boots on the bottom.

For some strange reason, she liked that.

"We're weeding all right. Bastard weeds. You ever seen stinging nettle?"

"No. That doesn't sound good."

"How about Jimson weed?"

"No, I get dandelions."

"Dandelions. For Christ's sake, those aren't weeds. They're food. They're edible. I'm talking about bastard, motherfucking weeds. Plants that try to kill you, poison you, shoot you with chemicals. This garden isn't some pansy-ass annual border with mari-fuckin'-golds. This is war. I've got weeds that try to strangle the other plants. I've got poison ivy that will send you to the ER. War. We're at Defcon One. Got it?"

Tom's face was so close, Bev could see every wrinkle around his eyes, every black and white whisker on his cheeks, a scar on his chin. She nodded. "Got it."

He looked pleased. "All right, then. Let's get to it. Follow me. I'll point out the hot spots." He grabbed her hand and led her through the garden gate. "This"—he ashed on a plant—"is stinging nettle. This is the worst. It shoots chemicals on you, and stings like a motherfucker. Do not touch it without your gloves."

"How does it shoot you? I don't understand."

"It's got hairs that are like needles, filled with chemicals. If you touch it the wrong way, it releases all sorts of good stuff, like histamine, acetylcholine—"

She gasped. "It looks so…so harmless. I can't believe it's capable of that."

"Don't be fooled by a harmless appearance. There are a lot of things in life that want to hurt you, Bev. Some are easy to spot. Some aren't." He paused and nodded at her neck. "You're not wearing your pearls today. That's good. Don't want to get your fancy jewelry covered with chicken shit."

"Why do you hate my pearls so much?"

They faced each other, still clutching hands.

"Because he gave them to you. And you were always so proud of them. And it pissed me off. That's the best he could do? A fucking strand of pearls? He was a piece-of-shit husband to you, but you were so easily placated by some jewelry, you didn't care? Jesus, Bev."

"I cared." Her throat hurt.

Tom took a step closer to her. "Did you?"

"It's the only thing of value that he ever gave to me. I know he gave her more. Probably jewels and clothing and trips." She tilted her chin. "Those pearls were it for me."

"You knew about her? I always wondered about that. If you knew."

"You knew?"

"Yeah. I knew. I saw them together."

She stumbled backwards, but Tom caught her by

the elbow.

"Steady there."

"You, you saw her? What did she look like? I knew her perfume. I could smell it on him when he got home. At first he would shower right away. After a while, he didn't even care about that. And neither did I. By that time he was sleeping in the guest room with the television going all night."

Tom scratched the back of his neck. "I saw them, but they didn't see me. She was trashy. Couldn't hold a candle to you. Roger was an idiot."

"Yes, well, perhaps *I* was the idiot. I stayed with him."

"No. You're not the idiot. Now you're free. What you decide to do with that…that either makes you an idiot, a coward, or someone a little bit fierce." He smiled at her. "Feeling fierce, Bev?"

Tom's eyes raked over her face, but for the first time his gaze felt gentle. She filed that interesting sensation away to explore later on.

"Me? Fierce?" Her laugh sounded strained. "Do I look fierce? I look like a tired old woman standing in a pile of chicken shit."

Tom's face broke into a huge grin. And then he started to laugh. He bent over at the waist and wheezed, with his hand on his knees. "Well, how about that? I got Miss Goody Two Shoes cussing."

Bev felt herself blush and rolled her eyes. "It's not that funny."

"Yep. It is." He glanced at something in the corner

of the plot. "Come here." Tom dragged her to the far end of the garden. He was still holding her hand. She liked his touch. It brought tears to her eyes.

"Look at that eggplant." He lifted the gigantic vegetable and hefted it in his hands, as though calculating the weight. "Do you know how to make eggplant parmesan?"

"Yes. I have a great recipe. Roger hated eggplant, so I hardly ever got to make it. Just for neighborhood parties."

Tom handed her the eggplant. "Roger was a douchebag." He leaned down to pick several more vegetables. "I'll go get the basket. Be right back."

She stood in the middle of the garden, her arms filled with purple eggplants, inhaling the scent of compost and earth and early morning sunshine.

The smell was growing on her.

FIVE

STRANGER THINGS
HAVE HAPPENED

"**Stop fidgeting**. It's not so bad." Tom squeezed a blob of first aid cream onto Bev's arm. "The sting will go away in a few minutes."

"I don't believe you." Bev's forehead furrowed in concentration.

He was so close to her, he could smell the detergent on her clothes and the shampoo she used. Tom liked a woman who looked her age. No plastic surgery, no plastic boobs, no plastic lips. In fact, hard to believe, Bev looked extremely fuckable at the moment. The tip of her nose was pink, her perfect hair had fallen into wispy chunks around her face, and her lips were rosy and plump. No hideous salmon-colored lip gloss today.

"I swear, sometimes I think that plant has a brain and a diabolical agenda." He could have stopped smoothing the cream on Bev's arm, but he didn't.

"What do you mean?"

"It shot you about one centimeter above the edge of your gloves. That's just plain diabolical. Motherfucking stinging nettle." Reluctantly, he stopped administering to Bev's rash. She'd been a trooper for over an hour. Weeding, collecting vegetables, re-mulching the paths.

He really wanted to fuck her.

"It feels like a bee sting." She blew on the red welts.

"I know. The good thing is it goes away pretty fast." Tom stared at her mouth.

"Tom? What are you looking at?"

"Uh. Nothing. Tell me what you need for the eggplant recipe. I'll pick it up for you at the store."

"Oh! I would love to go to the store. I need a few more things for Thanksgiving dinner."

He leaned forward and bit her bottom lip. It was just the right size. He hated women with thin, judgmental lips. Smeared with dark red lipstick. Stingy and manipulative. Bev's mouth looked ripe and vulnerable. He sucked on that soft lower lip for a few seconds.

He pulled back and laughed. Bev could not have looked more stunned if a leprechaun had come dancing into the kitchen.

"*What…are you doing?*" She barely got the words out.

"Kissing you." Tom leaned forward again and held the bottom of her chin. He worked his lips over hers until she responded. A soft whimper escaped her throat and he kept at it. Biting, sucking and finally spearing her mouth with his tongue. This was a wet motherfucking kiss.

"Oh." Bev placed her hand over his heart. She was shaking. "What are you doing, Tom? Have you lost your mind?" She stood up suddenly and backed away from him, until she hit the counter. The basket of eggplants tipped over and spilled on the floor. "Oh. My goodness!"

Tom followed her and pinned her against the counter. Her chocolate puppy dog eyes were dilated and confused. Her T-shirt was molded nicely to her chest. He wondered what her bra looked like.

"More." He kissed her again. This time just brushing his lips over hers. Her could feel her labored breathing, but he kept at it.

He slid his hands to her hips, grabbed on, and pulled her forward. Damn it if he wasn't turned on like a horny teenager.

"Tom!" Two sharp claws jabbed his arms.

"For the love of Christ." He took a step back and sighed. "You don't have to stab me."

"Yes, I think I do. You have clearly lost your ever-loving mind!"

Bev didn't realize it, but she looked adorable. Pink-cheeked, disheveled hair, swollen lips. For the first time, Tom got a peek of the woman underneath the hideous fucking salmon lip gloss.

And damn him for a fool, he liked what he saw.

Bev stared at his mouth. Then his eyes. Then his mouth. Back and forth. And just as he was about to remind her what French kissing was all about, a sharp rap on the front door interrupted them.

"Damn it," Tom growled. "Saved by the bell, Bev."

She looked equal parts relieved, disappointed, and totally confused.

He still wanted to fuck her.

"Excuse me! Anyone home!" A strange voice bellowed out front.

"Tom, someone's at your front door. Are you going to answer it?"

"Maybe they'll go away if I ignore them."

Bev poked him again with her talons. "That is rude. Go see who it is."

He grumbled as he pulled open the screen. "What?"

A father and son stood on his porch. The dad looked exhausted, sweaty and covered with dust bunnies and dirt. The little boy clutched his father's hand and gazed up into Tom's face with saucer-sized eyes.

"Do I know you?" Tom snapped.

The father held out his hand. "Jerome Franklin. I'm your new next door neighbor. This is my son, Jason. We just moved in yesterday. Hope we haven't been bothering you with the moving vans and ruckus."

Tom sighed. He shook the man's hand. "I'm sure

it will settle down soon."

"We're trying to get things in order before the holiday. We have family coming over." He patted the boy on his head. "Jason just learned to ride a two wheeler and he's raring to try it out, but he's got a flat, and I have no idea where the bike pump is." He raised an eyebrow at Tom. "Any chance you have a pump we could borrow? My wife just made some fresh lemonade. She's at home with our new baby. She'd like to meet you, too."

"Actually, I'm sort of busy right now." *Trying to seduce my son's mother-in-law.* "Not sure I have time to look around in the garage." He fiddled with the pack of cigarettes in his pocket.

The elder Franklin nodded. "Okay," he answered slowly. "We're sorry to bother you. I'm sure ours will turn up sooner or later."

Tom heard the baby crying next door.

The sooner he set limits with the new neighbors, the better. He didn't want them stopping by for a cup of motherfucking sugar. Or the kid selling magazines. Or them inviting him over for dinner. He liked eating alone.

He liked being left alone.

He glanced down at the boy. The kid was skinny as a twig and covered with bandages.

"Looks like you're taking your licks with the bike, huh?"

The kid took a step behind his dad's leg.

Jesus H. Christ.

The father chuckled. "Jason has a steep learning curve with the bike, it's true. But he's determined to master it. Right, Jay?"

The kid dug his fingers into his dad's pants.

Tom was pretty sure the bike pump was hanging next to the garage door. He shook out a cigarette from the pack.

"Learning to ride a two wheeler is pretty da— darned tough. I took a few spills in my day."

"That right?" Mr. Franklin lingered on the porch.

"Yep." Tom stuck the cigarette in his mouth, then glanced down at the boy. He sighed and put the cigarette back in his pocket.

"I got a tip for you, kid. Stay close to the edge of the street. If you think you're gonna fall, try to land on the grassy part, okay?"

The kid nodded.

"That's a good tip. Did you hear that, Jay? There's a lotta grassy front yards here." He turned back to Tom. "Our old place was in the concrete jungle. No soft landings there."

"Let me see if I can find the pump. I have an idea where it might be."

The kid smiled and hid his face completely behind the dad's legs. Little bugger.

"Thanks—I didn't catch your name."

"Tom. Jenkins." He grumbled under his breath.

"Nice to meet you, Tom. I appreciate the help with the bike."

Tom glanced back at Bev, who was watching

from the doorway. "This is Beverly, my...uh...son's mother-in-law." He stumbled over the words.

Jerome held out his hand to Bev. "Nice to meet you."

Beverly smiled. "It's very nice to meet you too. It must be hectic prepping for Thanksgiving and moving at the same time."

The dad laughed. "There's a lot of chaos at the house right now. We might need to get take-out."

"Beverly could donate a couple of dishes. She's been prepping for this dinner since the 1980s."

Tom wanted to laugh out loud at Beverly's incensed expression, but he kept a straight face.

"Wow. That would be great. You don't mind?" Jerome asked.

Beverly pasted on a fake smile. "No problem at all. We have a lot of food."

"We'll be over in a moment," Tom said.

The father and son left, and Tom leaned back on the porch railing. His eyes were glued to Bev whose lips were pinched together.

"Well, you were badgering me about getting chummy with the neighbors, so there you go. I did it. Now they'll be bugging the shit out of me for the next twenty years. Let's go find the bike pump and get a lemonade."

"I can donate a couple of dishes? As if I don't already have enough work to do for *our* Thanksgiving dinner. Tom!"

He cleared his throat. "I don't see what the trouble

is. Just double up on a couple of casseroles."

Beverly's eyes sparked. "Well, you should take the pump over. I'll be here. *Cooking*." There was practically smoke pouring out of her ears.

"Thanksgiving is two days away."

"Yes, and I'm way behind. I have pies and stuffing and—"

"You have plenty of time to do that later. You're the one who told me to be more neighborly, dammit. This is all your fault. Now you can just tag along and get a drink."

"I'm not thirsty."

He grabbed her hand again. She tugged and tried to pull away. He pulled her closer to him. "We're getting a lemonade.

Bev jabbed him with her fingernails. Stabbed him. He still didn't let go.

"You are infuriating."

"A lot of folks think that. Join the fucking club."

"Are you going to cuss like that in front of the children?"

He shrugged. "I'll try not to."

"It's disrespectful."

He nodded a couple of times. "Okay. Fair enough. I'll try to clean up my language. Happy?"

"Not even close."

He barked out a laugh. "You have a wicked sense of humor, Bev. Who knew?"

"I am not feeling in the slightest bit amused at the moment. You are nothing but a big bully, Tom

Jenkins."

"I can live with that." He let out a long sigh and squeezed her hand gently. "Come on, Bev. Don't make me go over there…alone."

All the tension in Beverly seemed to melt away. "I guess you don't make many social calls, do you? Feeling a little rusty?"

"Rusty enough to warrant a tetanus shot, probably."

Bev squeezed his hand back. She wasn't tugging anymore or trying to get away. That was good.

"Fine. I'll go. But I'll tell you something, Mr. Jenkins. *You* will be helping me with the extra casseroles."

He smiled.

She rolled her eyes.

They spent half an hour at the neighbor's house. He pumped up the flat bike tire and watched the little kid zoom around the neighborhood. Bev met the mom and patted the baby's back. When Jason smeared peanut butter all over Beverly's jeans, she hardly flinched. He caught her eye and shot her a wink.

She tried to suppress her smile, but failed.

All in all, it wasn't the worst experience of his life.

Six

Clean-up In Aisle Ten

Beverly surveyed the Hardin Market with a critical eye. It was perfectly functional, but nothing special. She really only needed odds and ends for her holiday meal, but she was planning to drag out this shopping event for as long as possible. Tom had pulled the rug out from under her, and it was not a comfortable feeling. He'd kissed her! Which wasn't the worst part.

The worst part was that she'd liked it.

She was used to Tom being an ass…rude and insulting. This new Tom—the one who revealed a vulnerable side, a sympathetic side, and most shocking to her, a sensual side—was throwing her for a loop.

The market was one place she had her bearings. Produce, dairy, baked goods. Everything had its place. Everything made sense. No surprises.

"So you see what you're looking for?"

Bev jumped and reached for her pearls. Her missing

pearls. She took a deep breath.

"Tom, I have asked you not to sneak up on me, please. Also, what are you doing here? I thought you were going to wait in the truck."

"I got bored. And I remembered a couple of things I wanted to get." He lifted a six-pack of beer.

She shook her head. "Thank goodness you didn't forget the beer. Thanksgiving would have been ruined."

"I know." Tom leaned against the cooler, looking like he didn't have a care in the world.

A plump middle-aged woman pushed her cart past Bev and glanced at Tom. "Well, Mr. Jenkins, how are you doing? Looking forward to Thanksgiving? Will you be seeing your son and his wife?"

Tom grumbled something under his breath.

"Mark and Celia are coming with all the grand-children! We can't wait to see them."

He shoved his hands in his pockets and looked at the squash.

"Well, it was nice talking to you. Hope you have a nice holiday." The woman smiled and continued on her way.

"Honestly, Tom, that wasn't very nice. That woman was attempting a conversation with you," Bev said, not bothering to cover up the disapproval in her voice.

"That woman never shuts up. If I had squeaked out even one word, I would still be here, three weeks after Thanksgiving Day. Believe me, the best way to discourage her is the silent treatment."

"Did it ever occur to you that having social inter-actions might actually be a nice change of pace? You just spent some time with your new neighbors and it didn't kill you, did it?"

He shrugged. "I'll bet you're in a knitting club. And a card club. And a birding club—"

Bev laughed. "Yes, I have some social clubs. I enjoy spending time with other adults."

"Well, I don't."

"You must have to deal with people for your job."

Tom tapped the cigarette pack in his front pocket. "Not too much. That's one of the reasons I like it. Folks tell me what they want, and then they leave me alone. I like the solitude of working on design projects."

She chose a large bunch of sage and stuffed it into a brown paper bag. "Is that why you left engineering to work as a contractor? I always wondered why. You spent so much time in school, and then didn't use your degree."

"I'll just bet old Roger had something to say about that." Tom shot her an icy look.

She was silent, waiting for his answer.

He picked up a gourd and tossed it into the air. "I didn't want to spend my days in an office, pushing pencils. Dealing with dumb-asses who wasted God-knows-how-much time running around trying to make decisions, scrambling on top of each other for promotions. Not my thing."

Bev nodded. "I understand. I can't imagine you

in a cubicle anyway. You're too…"

"Too what?" he asked.

"You just look like someone who needs to be active, outside, doing something…something practical, I guess." She bit her lip. "I…I still use the table you made for my garden studio."

"That old thing? That only took me about half an hour to whip up. I could make you something a bit more functional if you want. Something with cubbies, drawers. How do you use it?"

"I pot up my plants for the garden and organize my tools there." She smiled at him. "It's perfect, actually. Thank you."

Tom stared at her for a minute, saying nothing. The silence grew awkward. Beverly wasn't sure how to interpret his look, and she didn't have the courage to figure it out. If she calculated wrong, then he would snub her. Again. If she calculated right…that was even more intimidating.

An older gentleman walked by and said hello to Tom. He barely grunted a response.

Bev sighed. "I'm going to get a few more apples. We've been eating them and I need some more for the stuffing." She grabbed another paper bag.

"Get some Ginger Gold. I like those."

"I don't like yellow or green apples. Apples should be red."

"What? That is the dumbest thing I've ever heard."

"No, it's not. Green and yellow apples are too

tart, too mild. Red apples are the best."

"How about Granny Smith?"

"Too tart. Not enough sugar."

"How about Bramley?"

"Too sour. Ugh."

"Golden Delicious?"

"Mealy, no flavor."

"Dorset Golden?"

"No."

"Only red?"

"Yes, red." She slid several McIntosh apples into the bag.

Tom lifted a Newtown Pippin from the bin and removed a pocketknife from his jeans. He sliced a piece and popped it into his mouth.

"Tom! What are you doing? You haven't purchased that fruit."

He cut a small piece and held it to her mouth. "Try this."

Bev pursed her lips. "No, I—"

He took a step closer to her. "Try it, Bev. Just one bite."

She folded her arms across her chest. "Don't be ridiculous. I don't like those apples."

"This is good. Got a nice tang to it. Come on." He took the slice of apple and ran it along her lips.

She stopped breathing.

"Beverly Anderson, you're not afraid of a little yellow apple, are you?"

He was so exasperating!

Tom fed her the fruit. Standing there, in the middle of the produce section of Hardin Market, Tom Jenkins fed her a piece of apple, and Bev had an inkling what Eve felt like. Seduced by a plump, juicy fruit, by the touch of his hands, sweet and tart, sour and tangy.

This was ridiculous.

She swallowed. "Are you happy? I did it." Her gaze left his face and focused on the parsley behind him. She could feel her cheeks flaming.

"I'm getting a whole bag of green and yellow apples."

Her eyes shot back to his face, expecting to see a triumphant and gloating grin. But no. He looked determined. And something else she wasn't touching with a ten-foot pole.

"Fine. Waste your money. I'm getting red apples."

"Suit yourself."

When they got home, they filled up three enormous bowls with apples. Green, pink, golden, fiery red. The colors of autumn jewels.

Beverly would never admit it to the stubborn old goat, but she'd liked the Newtown Pippin.

Seven

Just Another
Pleasant Evening

The eggplant parmesan was perfect. Golden brown on the top. Cheesy and rich on the inside. Tom shoveled the meal into his mouth. When he cooked for himself, he made something simple like fried eggs. Or meatloaf. Which he could freeze for the rest of the week.

"Well, what do you think?" Bev asked. She stared at his near-empty plate. "Would you like seconds?"

"I'd like seconds, thirds, and fourths. This is delicious."

She beamed. "I'm so glad you like it. I haven't made this recipe for years. I guess I didn't forget how." She served him a huge portion.

"Thank you for cooking."

Bev looked startled. And then her eyes got suspiciously shiny. "Thank you for…thanking me." She took a ragged breath.

Tom wasn't sure what to say. "You're welcome."

Beverly fiddled with the napkin on her lap. "You must miss Alberta's cooking. She loved to putter in the kitchen. I remember."

He laughed. "Putter is a good word. She puttered in the kitchen, she puttered in the garden, she babbled on the telephone, she tinkered with her crafts projects. She puttered and babbled and tinkered."

Beverly slowly, deliberately, placed her fork on the table. "That wasn't very nice."

"What?" He wondered if there was any more garlic bread.

"Making fun of Alberta, when she isn't here to defend herself. She was a good wife to you."

Tom looked up and was surprised to see Bev seething with anger. "Just relax, Bev. Alberta did the best she could. But I'm being honest. She puttered. She babbled. I tuned her out most of the time. She meant no harm. We were just…well, I guess we had nothing in common."

"It's not easy being a wife and mother. It's exhausting. There's not a lot of energy left over to be scintillating and sexy and exciting. Someone has to clean the damned toilet. It's not sexy, but it needs to get done."

Her lips were pursed so tight, her jaw looked like it might crack.

Tom held up a restraining hand. "I appreciated the work Bertie did for me. Always. And I always helped out."

Bev slumped in her chair. "You're right. I know you did. You two had a good partnership."

"No, not really. We got stuff done around the house, but we never talked. She wanted to chat about her knitting project or a television show or her sister's new dog. Hell, she drove me batty. It wasn't that great, believe me."

"When did you two get married?"

"I was twenty six. She got pregnant the next year and had John."

"I married Roger right after college graduation. I was only twenty-one. I never even had my own apartment or job. My job was waiting on him." Bev took her fork and poked at the meal. "Do you think anyone has a good marriage? Really? Can you think of one?"

"Well, our kids seem to be doing okay."

She perked up. "That's true. They're actually good friends, aren't they?"

"Yep. They are." Tom swallowed another mouthful of casserole.

"Tom?"

"Yeah?"

"Aren't you lonely? I sometimes feel odd being alone in my big house. It echoes so much…all that empty space. If I didn't have my weekly activities, I'd go stir-crazy."

"Nope. Not lonely. I have work. I have chores. I don't bother anyone, and they don't bother me. That's the way I like it."

"Doesn't your neighborhood have a street party every fall? Did you help with that?"

"Don't get me started. Bunch of irritating house-husbands who don't know how to start a grill. They want me to loan them a table, and chairs, and a grill, and bring hamburgers, and make a bonfire for the kids. Bunch of moochers."

Beverly rolled her eyes. "For goodness' sake, Tom, not everything is a battle. Maybe your neighbors just wanted to see you and get to know you better."

She crossed her arms and surveyed him with a critical eye.

He didn't like it one bit.

"You know what your problem is?" she asked.

"I don't have a problem. And to be perfectly frank, I could give a shit what you think."

She continued on, ignoring his comment. "Your problem is you've turned into a hermit. You've isolated yourself. Alberta connected you to the community, and now that she's gone, you're all alone in this house. *Puttering.*"

Tom's left eyelid twitched. She'd put enough emphasis on the word "puttering" to piss him off.

She started it.

He would end it.

"Are you psychoanalyzing me, Bev? I didn't realize you got your degree in bullshit."

"That's why your front yard is a mess and so un-welcoming. You're trying to keep folks out. Why not invite them in and see what happens?"

"Should I call you Dr. Beverly now? Are you getting your own talk show soon?"

"Also, Tom, not everything is warfare. The garden is at Defcon One. The neighbors are a bunch of no-good moochers. Your poor late wife was a babbler who drove you crazy." She paused for effect. "You sure are hard to please."

"Well, at least I'm honest. And I don't pretend to be something I'm not. Ms. Stepford Wife with her perfect strand of pearls and manicured garden and bastard of a husband."

Her eyes narrowed. "You're a hermit. And you're scared. What are you scared of?"

He shoved a cigarette in his mouth. "I'm scared your motherfucking termites will never leave your house, and I'll be stuck with you forever. That's my biggest nightmare."

She smiled sweetly at him. "You're scared of being rejected. That's why you won't reach out to anyone."

He lit his cigarette angrily. "Your psychobabble is starting to get on my nerves, Bev. You're embarrassing yourself."

She shook her head. "No, no, I don't think I am. I think my observations are hitting just a little too close to home, and it's making you uncomfortable."

"You know what? I think that eggplant parmesan gave me indigestion. You need to work on that recipe." He stood up abruptly and pushed his chair back.

He stomped out to the porch, sat on the stoop, and took a long, hard drag on his cigarette.

Beverly Anderson was a pain in the ass and he was not the slightest bit interested in her evaluation of his life and shortcomings.

Too bad he couldn't stop thinking about that kiss and the little whimpers she'd made.

Damn him for a fool.

EIGHT

DAY THREE: GNOMES R US

"**You sure are** up early." Tom narrowed his eyes as Beverly nibbled on her morning toast. "I heard you take the car out. Where'd you go?"

Beverly tried to paste an innocent expression on her face. Tom slid a cigarette out of his pack and added hot water to the coffee grinds.

"Is that your breakfast every day? Coffee and cigarettes?"

"Yep. Breakfast of champions." His look dared her to comment.

She stayed silent and sipped her tea.

"So where'd you go?"

Bev cleared her throat. "I have a little project I'm going to be working on this morning. Then I'll start cooking this afternoon."

"Project? What sort of project?"

"Just something I think you'll like. In spite of yourself."

"Just what the hell is that supposed to mean? What are you planning, Beverly?"

She carried her dirty dishes to the sink. "Something to brighten up the front of your property. Make it look more welcoming and improve your curb appeal. Not scare off the new neighbors."

His cigarette almost fell out of his mouth. "Are you kidding me? What is this? A new reality TV show for HGTV? Fix up the old geezer's house? No thank you."

"I'll do all the work myself. I got delphinium and English daisies, some baskets of pansies for the porch. Compost…"

"Compost! I have enough compost in the back to fertilize the whole fucking state of California. You didn't need to get any compost."

Beverly folded her arms across her chest. "Well, I didn't think of that. I wanted to make sure I got everything I needed at the farm stand down the street. It's very sweet."

"I know it's *sweet*. But hell. I'm not interested in a home fucking makeover." He backed her up into the counter and scowled. "I've had just about enough of your helpful hints and suggestions and—"

Beverly saw a host of emotions on Tom's face. Anger. Irritation. And buried deep within his icy blue eyes, she saw just the slightest hint of curiosity. He might rail and yell and throw a fit, but down deep he was ready for a change.

Baby steps.

"Well. I'll tell you what. You can sit on the porch." She paused. "The stoop, I mean, and watch me work. Heckle me if you want to. Sip a lemonade while I do all the work. And when I'm done, if you hate it, you can rip the whole thing up and throw it in the compost pile."

Tom bracketed her with his arms on the counter. Now she was trapped. He leaned closer and stared at her mouth.

She was sure this was his idea of intimidation, but he had no idea how stubborn she could be. And this morning when she woke up—listening to the crows cawing on the telephone wires—she had a vision. Of his front porch looking sweet and lovely and welcoming.

And no matter how much he fought her, she was going to make that vision a reality.

"Me sit on the stoop and watch you sweat it out. There's a thought."

"See? You'll enjoy it."

He grunted. "You are the biggest pain-in-the-ass busybody I have ever goddamned met in my life."

She raised an eyebrow.

Tom backed up and swept an arm toward the front door. "Knock yourself out. But don't be surprised if the motherfucking daisies end up in the compost pile."

It was difficult, but Beverly only smiled on the inside.

He had to hand it to her. She was a hard-worker. And stubborn as a mule.

Tom guzzled a beer as he watched the sweat drip down Beverly's face.

She'd been at it for two goddamned hours. Ripping up weeds and edging a border in front of the porch. He didn't know squat about flowers. But it looked like she'd chosen some good ones. They seemed sturdy enough. And there were a lot of foliage plants, too. Maybe herbs, he wasn't sure. He hated to give her the satisfaction of asking about it. But at some point, he might just give in.

She stood, cracked her back, and wiped her forehead with a red bandana.

"Want a cold beer?" he taunted.

"No, thank you. I have water."

"Sure is nice in the shade."

She smiled. "I'm sure it is."

"Hope you didn't run into any poison ivy. That would put a damper on your holiday festivities."

"I'm being very careful, thank you. We're at Defcon Two this morning." She cocked her head to the side and shot him a fake smile.

Tom chuckled. He couldn't help himself.

Beverly tipped the wheelbarrow and worked her way over to the mulch pile at the edge of the driveway. She could barely maneuver it across the overgrown grass. He knew his scraggly lawn pissed off the neighbors. Which was why he ignored it. He had a state-of-the-art mower he used for the back.

Bev wrestled the wheelbarrow across the weeds, grunting as she hit a gnarled bunch of crabgrass.

"Goddammit to hell." He stood up reluctantly and headed to the garage. Five minutes later he roared into the front yard. He refused to look at her. She was kneeling in her garden plot, piling up mulch. He didn't need to look at her. He'd been watching for the last two hours. He knew exactly what she looked like.

Temptation.

He couldn't believe how badly he wanted to spank that sexy little ass in her faded blue jeans. Squeeze it and spank it and rub it. And bang it.

He wanted to bang Beverly Anderson.

Jesus H. Christ.

Tom mowed the entire front yard. And by the time he was done, he got a good view of Beverly's garden.

He hated to admit it.

Really hated to admit it.

But it looked good. Not prissy and pink and idiotic the way some gardens did. She'd chosen yellow and blue flowers and bunches of white daisies. They looked good with his green house. She'd tucked all kinds of foliage plants into the border. And hung pots from the old hooks on the porch.

"Well, what do you think? Is it going into the compost pile?" Bev blew out a long breath as she assessed her work. "By the way, thanks for mowing. Now I don't need to leave a bread crumb trail to find my way back through the forest."

"Not funny." Tom lit a cigarette.

"Hmm."

"What's that?" He pointed to a fragrant green plant.

"That's rosemary. I like to mix herbs into my borders. They smell nice, and they're practical." She glared at him. "I don't only use *nonessentials.*"

Tom cringed. "I said that, didn't I?"

"Uh huh."

"Did I sound like that big of a jackass when I said it?"

"Yes, you did."

Instead of apologizing, he pointed to another plant. "What's that over there?"

"Calendula. They're one of my favorites. The petals are edible."

"How much work is this gonna be? I don't feel like fussing with a bunch of flowers."

"Low maintenance. I put down a tarp with the mulch, so you shouldn't have any weeds."

"Well, it would be stupid to rip this up now. It would take me all afternoon. And…uh…the truth is…" He mumbled under his breath.

"What, Tom?" Beverly turned to face him.

"I guess I like it well enough. Doesn't look half-bad, not too prissy. I like the herbs, too." He ashed in the grass. "You did good work. I feel like a big asshole for watching you all day."

"You did mow down the forest."

"That I did."

"Oh wait! I forgot!" Beverly ran to the BMW and lifted something out of the trunk. She carried a small statue to the garden plot and placed it next to the stairs. It was one of those grumpy looking gnomes, with the pointy red hat and bright blue coat.

"What the fuck is that?"

She laughed. "It's you! I couldn't resist when I saw it at the farm stand. Look at his face. Doesn't he look cranky?"

Tom turned to Bev and started to laugh. He laughed so hard, it felt like he hacked up a lung. Beverly laughed harder. They had tears running down their cheeks as they stared at the gnome.

"Thank you. Beverly. Not for the gnome. For the rest of it."

"You're welcome."

"The gnome won't last twenty four hours. One of the druggie teenagers will steal it. Guaranteed."

"That's okay. I got it on sale."

He reached over and grabbed her hand. He lifted it for inspection. Small and soft. "You broke a nail. You broke a nail for this garden. Was it worth it?"

"It was worth it. It was worth seeing you laugh, and knowing you like it. Even though that probably killed you to admit it."

"Yup."

She looked down at her hand, still clutched in his. "Maybe it's time to trim my nails. I guess that would make life a little bit easier."

"I approve of that decision. I'm tired of you stabbing the shit out of me."

They laughed again.

Tom sighed. "Just so you know, it's not going to change anything. I'm not planning to host any neighborhood parties with fucking Ritz cracker snacks. I just like how it looks."

"Okay. That's good enough for now."

NINE

ALL HELL BREAKS LOOSE

Beverly was ready to cook. She had a station laid out for stuffing. A station for the broccoli casserole. A station for potatoes and yams. And a station for pies. Each area had cutting boards, the proper ingredients pre-measured, and plastic containers for storage. Tomorrow she would pop everything into the oven just before Karen and John arrived, so it would be piping hot and perfect.

Thanksgiving would be perfect.

"You should have gone into the military, Bev. You would have made a good general." Tom's gaze raked over the kitchen with amusement. "Your attention to detail is terrifying."

"Yes, well, I'm not much for flying-by-the-seat-of-my-pants with party preparation. I have a system, and it works for me," she said.

"Your system scares the shit out of me. What

happens if something goes wrong?"

Bev stiffened. "Wrong? What could possibly go wrong?"

"I don't know. The oven breaks, the milk goes bad, the pies burn. What happens to your *system* if there's a melt-down?" Tom asked.

"I don't have melt-downs," she answered. "If you're here to help, wonderful. If not, you should sit out on the stoop for a few hours. I need to get everything chopped, mixed, assembled, and packed for tomorrow."

Tom grunted. "Fine. I'm out of here. I don't want to disturb your system." He grabbed a rolled up newspaper and a beer from the fridge.

Thirty minutes later, Bev inspected her work with pride. Mounds of chopped celery, onions, and apples decorated the counter. She was just about to start chopping herbs when she heard voices on the front porch. Tom entered the kitchen with Mr. and Mrs. Franklin and their two children.

"Bev, you remember the new next door neighbors?" He nodded at the family.

"Of course." She wiped her hands on her apron. "How are you doing?"

Lily, the mom, shifted the baby to her shoulder and sighed. "Not too good. Our range is broken and we have five pies to bake for Thanksgiving. I was just asking Mr. Jenkins if he could spare a few hours of cooking time in his oven. Otherwise I don't know how we're going to get all this done." The baby gurgled and tugged on her hair.

"It sure smells good in here. You're already cooking for tomorrow?" Jerome asked. His little boy reached up a hand to snag a piece of chopped apple. Beverly had to restrain herself from slapping the table with her wooden spoon.

"Yes, I am. I have quite a few dishes to prepare…"

Tom leaned back on the counter. "I don't think Bev is doing any actual cooking yet. Just chopping stuff up. I don't see why you couldn't throw your dessert in the oven."

Bev counted silently to ten. "There's not a lot of room in here to work—"

Lily smiled. "Oh, no problem. I'll get these in and out of the oven as fast as possible. Thank you so much. I know our Thanksgiving dinner isn't going to be a gourmet meal, by any means, but I would at least like to have the pies done."

Jerome draped an arm around his wife's shoulders. "We'll help and try to get this finished as soon as possible. Then get out of your hair."

Mr. Franklin took a tray loaded with pies and set it on the counter. Bev watched as the scene unfolded in slow motion. The tray smacked the glass jar stuffed with sage. The jar teetered, and toppled. Rivulets of water streamed along the marble and dripped onto the floor. The sage lay in a puddle, and mini tributaries branched out to soak her crisp vegetables and recipe cards.

In with the good air.

Out with the bad air.

"Whoops. I'll get that." Tom tugged a rag from the basket and threw it down, then wiped up the spill with his boot. He shot Bev a smile.

She sent him a pleading look. *Please don't let them stay.*

He raised an eyebrow. *It was your idea to get chummy with the neighbors.*

"Well, this should be nice and cozy. I'll go sit out on the stoop and finish my beer. Good luck in here." Tom whistled on his way out the door. Whistled! Beverly wanted to pick up the glass jar and fling it at his head. She took a deep breath, pasted a fake smile on her face, and pushed her stuffing station into the corner.

"Is this enough room for you to spread out?" There was a slight tremor in her voice, but hopefully the Franklins didn't notice.

"Yes, thanks again, Beverly." Lily pulled out her pies and lined them up on the counter. The baby leaned over and drooled on the cutting board.

Bev wondered where Tom kept his aspirin.

He gave them an hour.

He knew Beverly was seething in the kitchen. Her perfect little system was probably all bent out of shape. While he waited, neighbors walked down the street and shouted hello. Said they liked the new garden.

Asked about his family. Asked about his holiday plans.

Beverly had cut away his protection from the rest of the world.

Even the hipsters had stopped by to chat. They were walking a bunch of hipster dogs and smelled like marijuana.

He raised the newspaper to shield his face, but they were undeterred. Everyone seemed so damned perky today, it was irritating as hell. After an hour of forced conversation and greetings, he decided to see how Bev was faring in the warzone.

Tom was prepared to laugh, but the look on her face stopped him short. She was wound up tight and ready to crack. The well-organized kitchen had dissolved into flour spills on the counter, a baby crawling on the floor, pies all over the table, and Jason dancing around the room. The Franklins seemed totally oblivious to the fact that Beverly was primed for a nervous breakdown. Her shoulders were hunched over and she flinched every time the little kid screamed. Which was a lot.

The beautifully orchestrated stations no longer existed. It looked like the Franklin family had usurped the battlefield, and Bev had been sent to the outskirts.

"Anybody home?" The screen door squeaked and slammed shut as Paul DiBenedetto—Tom's nudist neighbor—sauntered into the kitchen. As luck would have it, fully clothed.

"I smelled something good outside. Pies?"

"Do you always walk uninvited into other folks' homes?" Tom barked.

Paul shrugged. "No, but I figured you were turning over a new leaf with the landscaping. And visitors. And cooking." He eyed the pies.

Tom reluctantly introduced the Franklins and DiBenedetto. Beverly barely nodded. Her gaze darted to the door.

"I'm a bachelor. Hardly ever get homemade cooking."

Tom wouldn't have been surprised to see drool on Paul's chin as he examined the food.

"Tell you what." Tom shook a cigarette out of the pack and reached for Bev's hand. She relinquished it without a fight. It looked like the fight had gotten squashed right out of her.

"Bev and I are going to get some fresh air. Why don't you all clean up in here, take the pies back to your place, and enjoy a snack? We have guests on the way and need to get ready for our holiday plans." He didn't feel in the slightest bit guilty about stretching the truth.

Tom had officially reached his limit for social bullshit.

Without waiting for an answer, he pulled Beverly out the back door and over to the vegetable garden. He continued to hold her hand as he led them to a path between the cabbage and onions.

"Hey."

Her eyes were shell-shocked. "Hey," she whispered. Tears leaked down the side of her face.

"Come on, Bev. It's not so bad. We'll clean it up and get back on track. Back on your system. Everything's gonna be fine."

"No, it won't." Her voice cracked. "I wanted it to be perfect. For Karen! This is the first Thanksgiving since Roger died and I need it...want it...to be..." She hiccupped and took a deep breath. "I want her to see I'm okay without him. Everything's the same. Fine."

Tom dropped his cigarette butt to the ground and stomped on it. He slid his arms around Bev's waist and pulled her close. "Beverly. Karen doesn't care if the dinner is perfect. She just wants you to enjoy yourself. For Christ's sake, it's no secret that Roger treated you like crap for almost forty years. Karen just wants you to be happy. She could give a shit if there's sweet potato pie for Thanksgiving."

"I won't let him win. If...if...the dinner is bad, he wins."

"Bull. And shit. What the hell are you talking about?"

Beverly shook so badly, Tom thought she would faint. He pulled her tightly against him, hoping some body heat would thaw her out. "He's not gonna win, Bev. You win. You're alive and doing your thing, and he's gone. You can't go back and relive the last thirty-some years, but you can damn well live your life now anyway you want to." He stepped back just enough to look into her pretty brown eyes. She blinked and tears clung to her lashes. Jesus. This was killing him.

"You hear what I'm saying? You won."

She gazed up into his face and startled him by touching his chin. "I like your whiskers. Roger didn't like that scruffy look. He said it was dirty. He was always so primped and doused with cologne. Prissy." She forced a crooked smile. "Just like the flowers you don't like." She stroked his chin, over and over, and Tom had the irrational urge to fling her to the ground of his garden.

She leaned against him and rested her head on his shoulder. "This dinner is going to be a disaster."

"No, it's not. We've got beer and a big-ass turkey to cook. I'll do that. I'll rustle up a nice gravy. It will be fine. Believe me."

"I'm hungry. Do you think…those people are gone? I wouldn't mind getting a snack. Maybe a glass of wine."

Tom pressed his mouth against the top of her head and smiled. "Now you're talking. Let's get a drink and some cheese and crackers and take a load off. There's plenty of time for cooking later."

Beverly grabbed onto his biceps and squeezed. *Christ, that felt good.* She shot him a sheepish look. "I hate to admit it, but that whole scenario was pretty much my biggest nightmare. Strangers ruining my plans. I felt out of control, angry, and I always have to be polite. I can't ever say what I really think."

"Of course you can. Say no. Go ahead and say it.

No."

"No."

They both laughed. "See. You can do it. Not so hard."

"You always say what you think. It must be incredibly liberating to do that all the time."

"I don't think about it. I just do it. Pisses folks off, but who gives a shit?"

"Aren't you worried about hurting someone's feelings?"

"Not really. Are you?"

"Yes. I guess I am. I don't want anyone to think I'm rude."

"What about *your* feelings? I think it's time to start worrying about your own damned feelings, Beverly. Roger is gone. The only one you have to please now is yourself."

"I don't have the faintest idea where to even start." Tears started to flow again.

Tom cupped her face. "No more crying. You know where to start. What's something you always wanted to do? Something you put off. Something Roger wouldn't approve of." He smoothed the tears away with his thumbs and kissed the corners of her eyes.

What the fuck was wrong with him?

"A garden tour." Her voice was hoarse.

"Okay."

"In England. The English countryside. Just milling about and seeing the flowers. Roger made fun of me.

Said it was a ridiculous idea and a huge waste of money."

"Fuck him. You're going."

Her laughter sounded light.

"I am?"

"Yep. You're going. You're gonna dance with the daisies."

Then she really laughed.

He felt heroic. God help him, he wanted to make her laugh again. That laugh was light and golden and free.

"If it makes you feel any better, I just got to live my biggest nightmare too." He brushed his whiskers against her soft cheek.

She raised her eyebrows. "What's that?"

"Since you fixed up the front of my house, I can't hide behind the tall grass anymore. All my neighbors want to…chat."

She giggled. "Uh-oh."

"Oh yeah. Chat. And shit, it's killing me. I hope you're happy." He rubbed her back, along the bony ridge of her spine. She sighed, so he figured it was all good.

Beverly peered up at him. "Well, you're still standing so I guess you survived."

"Barely. Between the chatting neighbors in the front, and the annoying neighbors in the kitchen, and goddamned DiBenedetto showing up—thank God with his clothes on—I've had just about enough."

Bev nodded. "Me too." Her arms had wrapped

around his waist, and now her soft little hands were stroking his back. Over his dingy white T-shirt.

It felt like heaven.

It felt like hell.

"Let's open up that bottle of Coppola Merlot. I need a drink."

Tom smiled. "Now that's the best goddamned idea I've heard all day. Let's go."

TEN

SO THAT'S WHAT THEY WERE TALKING ABOUT

The kitchen.

Oh God! The kitchen.

Bev squeezed her eyes shut and made three wishes. Maybe it would work.

When she opened her eyes the kitchen was still a mess. She whimpered.

"Bev?"

Sniff.

"What? This isn't so bad. They cleaned up and went away. That's what you wanted, right?"

"This is clean?" Beverly winced at the shrillness of her voice.

"Looks pretty good to me."

"Clearly you and I have different standards for cleanliness."

He chuckled. "I promise I'll help get your stations

reorganized later. Come on. Let's go into the living room with some cheese and crackers and wine."

She nodded. She was afraid if she opened her mouth to answer, she would wail.

Tom tugged her into the living room. He thrust a giant glass of red wine into her hands and pushed a plate of food to the edge of the coffee table.

"Eat that. You're getting shaky. You need some food."

Beverly looked down at the plate. Ritz crackers, pre-sliced cheese, and a few strawberries. She took a big sip of her wine as she settled on the couch.

"Are these from the farm stand?" She picked up a berry and nibbled.

Tom sat across from her and poured himself a bourbon. "Yep, they're good. How about we serve turkey and strawberries tomorrow?"

Bev laughed. She couldn't help it. Tom sure was trying hard to cheer her up.

She bit into the strawberry and focused on that one bite. Sweet, juicy, simple. Why did Thanksgiving have to be so complicated?

She let out a long sigh. "I'll take care of it tomorrow morning. The cleaning, the cooking. I just can't face everything right now. I'll do it in the morning."

"No."

Bev glanced up to see Tom looking more irritable than normal.

"What do you mean *no*?"

"Sorry, Bev, but you're not doing all this by

yourself. The cleaning. The cooking. I'm helping whether you like it or not. You might not approve of the way I do things, but I'm officially your partner-in-crime for Thanksgiving. Got it?"

She took another generous sip of wine. "I'm not used to…you know. Having a partner."

"I know. Roger watched TV while you worked your ass off. I noticed." Tom sipped his bourbon.

"Well. That's how it was."

"That's how it was with him, because he was a royal douchebag. Bertie and I always divvied up the chores for holidays. I might not be Miss Fancy Pants Martha Stewart, but I manage to feed myself on a daily basis." He reached across the table and squeezed her hand. "Partners."

How tempting to share the burden. How tempting to let down her defenses. To let Tom in. Did she dare?

"I can only imagine what you would prepare for Thanksgiving."

Tom chuckled. "How do you feel about beer can turkey on the grill?"

Bev barked out a half laugh/half cry and spit out the berry. It landed on the table, right next to her plate. Horrified, she covered her mouth. "Excuse me." She could feel her cheeks flaming.

She reached over with a napkin to pick up the offending piece of food, but Tom beat her to it. He snatched it up and popped it into his mouth.

"Well, isn't that tasty?" He chewed the strawberry slowly and smiled at Beverly.

Her mouth hung open, stunned into silence.

"No use wasting a perfectly good strawberry," he said.

"Tom! You are insane! That is…that is…I don't even know what to say. I spit that out!"

"So what. I've already been inside your mouth." The heated look he sent her shocked her senseless.

Beverly didn't think it was possible, but she felt her blush intensify.

"That is…oh my God!"

He stood up and took another gulp of bourbon. Then moved to the sofa and sat down perilously close to her, crowding her into the corner.

"Tom? What are you doing?" She could feel the heat of his leg pressed up against her. Hard as a rock.

"I'll bet you taste like strawberries. Do you taste like strawberries, Beverly?"

She made the mistake of looking into his eyes. Not so icy blue anymore. His face was too close. She caught her breath as he licked his lips.

"Are you flirting with me? Because this is utterly ridiculous."

His hand landed on her leg and rubbed up and down her slacks. The sight of his dark rough fingers clutching the silky fabric was mesmerizing. He squeezed her thigh. A heaviness, a fullness, seeped into the space between her thighs, the space she'd ignored for thirty-seven years. *This cannot be happening.*

"How am I doing? I'm a little bit rusty with the whole flirting thing," Tom said, his voice scratchy.

"I have no idea. I need to go clean the kitchen." She started to get up, but he pushed her down.

"Not yet. I want to taste you. I want some more strawberries."

Tom leaned over and kissed her. Nipped at her lips, moaned as his tongue slid into her mouth. He was so very different from Roger. She had no idea how to respond. She lifted her hand and stroked his cheek. The pads of her fingers dragged over the stubble and she nipped back at his top lip. *I hope I'm doing this right. The way he likes it.*

"Oh fuck, that's it. Don't stop, Bev."

I guess he likes it.

"Better than strawberries."

She shivered as his hands roamed. His beard rasped her neck.

"You like this don't you, Miss Prim and Proper?"

"I…I don't know."

"I think you do. I'm gonna enjoy every second of watching you come undone."

It was the wine. It was the exhaustion. Things were uncertain. Up in the air.

It was his touch. Rough and gentle. It was his mouth. Biting, sucking.

If she closed her eyes, she could be anyone. Someone else.

They made out on the sofa. Like a couple of kids. She was melting into a puddle. Like a slab of brie on a platter, bubbling under the broiler.

His hands cupped her breasts, stroked between

her thighs, snuck under her blouse. She could feel the lift of her hips, searching for his hardness. He pressed her down on the sofa and ground against her, relieving the ache. Her nails scored his back and he sucked hard on her neck.

She whimpered. "Oh my God. That feels good."

"What feels good? What? This?" He pushed his erection against her. "Or this?" He nibbled and sucked on her neck.

"Both," she whispered. "Both. Everything. I think I'm drunk."

"The hell you are. You're turned on."

He lifted his head and gazed into her face. They were both breathing hard. "Have you ever been aroused like this before, Beverly?" He rolled his hips over her and she cried out.

"No." She was so embarrassed, tears formed in her eyes.

"There's nothing to worry about. I'm gonna make you feel good, okay?"

"I'm too old for this."

"Bullshit. You're only fifty-nine. Why do you keep calling yourself old?" He removed her blouse and nuzzled her cleavage. "Look at these sweet little titties. They're perfect."

"You are insane." She would die if he stopped. Die.

He unsnapped her bra and sucked on her nipples. Back and forth, over and over again. Beverly was vaguely aware she was bucking up against him, arching her back. The noises she made didn't sound human.

"You like that, don't you?" Tom appeared entirely too pleased with himself.

She nodded. "Do I get a turn?" Her voice was shaky.

He laughed. "Christ, I sure hope so. I'm about to explode."

"Are we going to have sex on the sofa?" Bev blurted it out.

"Yep, we sure are." He pulled off his clothes and flung them to the floor. He gently removed her slacks and underwear, then dragged his rough hands all over her skin.

She was having sex with her daughter's father-in-law. On the sofa.

Oh my God!

She watched in a daze as he lowered himself onto her. Big, hot, naked man, hard and heavy and sexy. The look in his eyes as he absorbed every detail was stunning. He didn't look bored, or disgusted.

He looked excited. He looked hungry.

Tom propped himself up on his elbows and rubbed his thick erection over her slickness. Had she ever been wet like this? Her brain wasn't functioning. Something was winding tight inside of her. Hot and melted, bubbling. Sizzling. This was it. How it was supposed to feel.

"Honey, don't cry." Tom kissed the corner of her eyes.

"I didn't know," she sobbed.

"It's okay. It's gonna get better. Just relax and let go." He rubbed and rubbed and entered her and moved. Beverly moved too. Not in the least bit self-conscious.

In the morning she would pretend this was all a dream.

"That's my girl. Give me a ride." Tom's breathing fractured in her ear. He shouted and slapped his pelvis against her.

She moaned as he sucked her breasts again and something rushed up inside of her, tortured and ready. Waiting for years, waiting for him.

They erupted together, glued to each other with sweat and heat pooling beneath them.

"That's my girl." He kissed her forehead. He kissed the tip of her nose. He kissed her cheeks, wet with tears.

"Oh. My. God."

"Was that your first orgasm, Bev?"

She nodded, afraid to speak.

"Ready for the second one?"

Thomas Jenkins had a twinkle in his eye. Like a mischievous teenager, raring to go.

Her partner-in-crime. On the sticky sofa.

"I'm ready," Beverly said.

ELEVEN

THANKSGIVING DAY

"**Well, the house** is still standing." John hefted a box of beer in his arms as he jogged up the steps to his dad's porch.

"I'm just worried. I tried calling my mom about a thousand times this morning and didn't get an answer. That's weird." Karen cradled a stuffing casserole. "Why wouldn't she answer?"

John laughed. "Are you kidding me? She is probably running around like a crazy person making sure every last detail is perfect. You know your mom." He swung open the porch door with his foot. "Dad! We're here."

Karen and John stepped into the foyer and placed their boxes on the floor. "Mom!" Karen yelled. "Oh my God. Maybe they killed each other! We're going to find dead bodies, I know it." She bit her lip.

"Huh. That is sort of odd." John peeked into the

living room. "Oh fuck me." He took a step back. "Karen, don't go in there."

"Are you kidding me? Dead bodies?"

"No. Live bodies." John started to laugh.

"What is so funny?" Karen demanded and stomped over to the living room entrance. She stopped in her tracks and then began to slowly shake her head back and forth. "That's not...possible. Not...no. No. Absolutely...No."

John grabbed her hand and pulled her back to the foyer. His wife's face was white. "Let's give them some privacy, okay?"

"John." Her voice trembled.

"Yes, sweetheart?"

"Um, I did not just see our parents on the sofa. Naked, under a blanket. With their arms around each other. Naked. Together." Her eyes were wide. "Naked."

"How about that? They didn't kill each other." John stroked her back in a soothing motion. He was trying like hell not to laugh again.

"John." Her breath was labored.

"Uh-huh." He couldn't help himself. He started laughing.

"This is *not* funny! Not! Our parents hate each other. Your dad hates everyone! It's not even possible in an alternate reality." She bent over, trying to catch her breath. "Oh my God!"

"Jesus H. Christ! Who's making such a racket out there! We're trying to—" John heard his dad yell, and then some rustling from the other room.

Karen and John listened to the whispered conversation in shock.

"Bev, don't be embarrassed."

"I can't believe we slept so late! I haven't even cleaned up, or started dinner…"

"I told you not to worry about that. We'll all pitch in."

"Tom, help me find my clothes."

"I don't want to…"

"Now!"

John recognized that tone of voice. When Bev barked out an order like that, she meant business.

"I like you naked," Tom said.

If possible, Karen's face became paler.

"Tom, stop that!" Mrs. Anderson giggled.

John and Karen had been married for five years, and never, not once, had he heard Mrs. Anderson giggle. Not even close.

John shook his head. "That's it. We're out of here." He led Karen right out the door to the front porch. She staggered outside. "Dad! We'll wait in the car until you're ready for us." He held Karen's hand and steered her to the back of the Volkswagen.

"Hon."

Karen nodded. She seemed incapable of speech.

"It's not that bad."

"Really? It's not? I'm thinking this heralds the commencement of the zombie apocalypse or something."

John kissed her cheek. "Did you see them snuggled

up together? They looked happy. My dad's been lonely for a long time. Your mom…she deserves some fun."

She slowly nodded her head. "I agree with both of those things. Your dad is lonely, but he also pushes people away. In spectacular fashion. My mom…I just can't believe she had *fun*"—she cringed when she said the word and John snorted against his will—"with your dad."

He coughed. "You know what I noticed?"

"What?" She plunked her head down on his shoulder and sighed. "What did you notice? That the entire world just tipped on its axis and we've entered a rip in the space-time continuum?"

"God, I love being married to a sci-fi geek. That really turns me on, babe."

She laughed and punched him in the arm.

"No, that's not what I noticed. What I noticed was they were both smiling. In their sleep."

She raised her head and looked at him. "They were."

"Uh-huh. Smiling." He struggled to avoid another round of laughter.

"Oh my God!"

Karen was convinced.

It *was* a rip in the space-time continuum.

She watched in complete amazement as her mother chopped apples—gold and green apples, no less—and put them in a bowl. Her mom wore faded jeans, one of Tom's old T-shirts, and not a speck of make-up. Or jewelry. The pearls were missing in action. Her fingernails were no longer daggers.

Tom kissed the back of her mom's neck and Bev closed her eyes. In a sweet, relaxed moment of bliss. She couldn't hide it.

Holy crap on a cracker, her mom was falling in love with Tom Jenkins.

If a comet filled with aliens exploded directly into the kitchen, Karen would not be more surprised.

Bev picked up a cube of apple and popped it into Tom's mouth. He looked at her with complete focus and intensity, his bright blue eyes blazing. And then he leaned down and gave her a kiss right on the lips. A hot kiss.

Karen's mom blushed and kissed him back.

"Karen? You've been washing that head of lettuce for about ten minutes. I'm pretty sure it's clean by now." John gently removed the greens from her hands and set them on the counter. "You okay, hon?"

She nodded.

"You sure? How about a glass of wine?"

She nodded harder.

"I'll get you the wine. Babe?"

Karen turned to John and tried to ignore the parental drama in the background.

"It's gonna be okay."

She faced her husband, who wasn't even trying to hide the smirk on his face. "If you say so."

"Karen, can I help you with the salad?" Her mom suddenly materialized next to her. "I am so embarrassed Thanksgiving dinner isn't ready. Forgive me?"

Her mother looked so nervous it broke Karen's heart.

"Mom, I don't care about the dinner. It's no big deal. We have plenty of food."

"Tom said you'd feel that way. I…" Her mom pursed her lips. "I felt like I had to produce a perfect dinner, just the way we used to have with your dad. I don't want you to think that since your father has died I'm some sort of slacker or something."

Karen shook her head in disbelief. "God, I wish you'd be a slacker for a while. There's no reason to spend so much time creating a decorator showcase house and garden and meals. Just relax." She glanced at Tom who nodded at her in solidarity.

I can't believe I'm thinking this, but I actually have a feeling Tom Jenkins is good for my mother. Holy Crap!

"I had everything under control yesterday, and then some neighbors came over—"

"—and all hell broke loose. Bev doesn't do so well when her system is fucked up."

Bev glared at Tom.

He cleared his throat. "Excuse my French. Screwed up. I meant screwed up."

John laughed so hard he started wheezing.

Karen slid her arm around Bev's waist. "It's okay. I sort of like doing this hodgepodge dinner. It's fun." She kissed her mom on the cheek. "Although I do think I need more alcohol."

"Me too." Her mom kissed her back, and the two of them smiled at each other.

Are you sure you know what you're doing? Sleeping with Tom Jenkins?

I like him. I think he likes me, too.

"Ladies, please enjoy this fine Merlot, compliments of your host." Tom offered both of them a glass of wine and tossed a beer can to his son.

Bev took a big gulp of her wine. "Well, I've never had such a ramshackle Thanksgiving meal before, but I guess we won't starve. Every time I look around this room and see the mess and willy-nilly organization, I…" She glanced at Tom. "I feel like I'm jumping out of an airplane without a parachute."

Tom removed the glass from Bev's hands and pulled her into his arms. "I'll catch you. Don't worry."

Karen turned her face away from them so they wouldn't catch the tears in her eyes. John hugged her from behind and whispered, "I told you it was gonna be okay."

She let the tears fall. "I do believe you may be right."

"Those goddamned kids. They stole my gnome." Tom scowled with his hands on his hips and glared at the empty spot in his garden. "I knew it! Not even twenty-four goddamned hours."

John settled down on the stoop with his plate of food and peered at the garden. "Is that new? I don't remember you having flowers in the front." He frowned. "I don't remember you having anything in the front. Except tick grass."

Karen sat one step up from her husband and set her plate and glass of wine on the porch. "It looks great, Tom."

Tom grunted. "Your mom did it. Got a bee in her bonnet about me being a hermit." He held out a hand to Bev. "Can I help you sit on the stoop? How are your knees this morning?"

Bev grasped his hand. "Thank you. I can't believe we are eating Thanksgiving dinner on paper plates, on the stoop. Martha Stewart would *not* approve."

He sat down next to her and slid over until their hips touched. All he could think about was holding onto her naked hips and whispering dirty talk in her ear. Who knew Miss Prim and Proper could be so sexy and shy and sweet at the same time?

Miss Prim and Proper hadn't been so proper last night.

"I'm digging this anti-Martha meal," John said. "Beer can turkey on the grill, strawberry salad. Budweiser. I'm in heaven." He dunked a piece of turkey into the gravy pool on his plate.

"I think we should start a new family tradition," Tom said. "Thanksgiving on the stoop."

"With canned gravy and canned cranberry sauce," added Karen.

"My mother is turning over in her grave." Bev sighed. "But I have to admit everything is delicious."

"Especially the apple stuffing. Made with green and gold apples." Tom taunted Bev with a raised eyebrow.

"Yeah. I noticed that," Karen said. "My mom has a thing about red apples. How'd you get her to try the other colors?"

Bev rolled her eyes. "He harassed me until I gave in and admitted they were tasty. Maybe I was too adamant about the whole apple rule."

"Maybe." Tom jammed a forkful of stuffing into his mouth. "Jesus, this is good. Nice job, Bev."

She beamed. Again. Tom swore she was glowing a bit this morning.

"Thank you, Tom."

"Hey, Dad, looks like the neighbors are coming over for a visit." John gestured to the Franklins who traipsed across his freshly mowed lawn, bearing pies.

"Remind me why we mowed the grass again?" Tom asked, glaring at Beverly.

"It won't kill you to say hello," she answered.

"We're eating our holiday meal, for Christ's sake." He grumbled under his breath. "How long do you think it will take to regrow that grass four feet high?"

Beverly laughed.

"Happy Thanksgiving." Jerome waved in greeting. Bev made introductions while the new neighbors took seats on the porch steps.

"Our family will be here in an hour or so, but we wanted to thank you for the use of your kitchen yesterday."

Jerome handed a pie to Bev. "I hope you didn't mind our interference. This is one of Lil's pecan pies. Really good. With bourbon in it."

Bev nodded politely. "Thank you."

About fourteen seconds later Paul DiBenedetto showed up, with a transparently innocent expression on his face.

"Time for pie?"

Tom shot Bev a sullen look. "Maybe I could plant a stinging nettle garden in the front. What do you think of that?"

She clasped his hand and kissed it. "I'm proud of you, Mr. Hermit. In the immortal words of a wise man, *everything's gonna be fine.*"

"If he's so damned wise, why doesn't anyone ever listen to him?" And just because he could, and he wanted to, and he was still feeling irked and somewhat sorry for himself, he leaned over and kissed Beverly Anderson on the mouth.

With tongue.

Within half an hour, the hippies from the corner were making small talk with the Franklins, their pissy little dogs were sniffing around Bev's new garden, and the idiot down the street who'd fallen off the trellis was hobbling over in his brand new cast with a platter of food.

Tom whispered in Beverly's ear "Did I put a sign on the front lawn that says *please bug the holy living shit out of me, I like it*? 'Cause I don't remember doing that."

Bev laughed so hard, her shoulders shook.

The kid handed him some cookies.

"What's this?" Tom asked, confused.

The kid shrugged. "My mom wanted to thank you for helping out with her stone fence a couple of months ago. She said it fell down in the road and you rebuilt it. And didn't charge her."

Tom waved a hand. "That was nothing. I like stonework." He peeked under the foil. "What kind of cookies?"

The kid smiled. "Ginger. They're really good dunked in milk."

Jason Franklin shuffled over the step. "I like cookies."

Tom handed him the plate. "Knock yourself out, kid."

It took two hours before the crowd dispersed. How the fuck his house had turned into Grand Central Station, he had no bloomin' idea. But he tuned out most of the ruckus. He was focused on Beverly. Her smile. Her hand casually rubbing his back. Her blush when he kissed her.

He wasn't too proud to admit he'd underestimated Beverly Anderson.

Tom found DiBenedetto in the backyard, investigating his vegetable garden.

"You need something, Paul?"

Paul looked shocked. "You offering? You never offered me anything before."

"Maybe. Maybe we can make an exchange."

DiBenedetto looked dubious. "What are you talking about?"

"You're a travel agent, aren't you?"

He nodded. "Yes, I am."

"I need a couple of tickets. Can you print them up today?"

"Sure. I can do it on my home printer." Paul pointed to a row of cabbages. "I'll tell you what. You give me three of those nice purple cabbages, and I'll get you the tickets. What do you say?"

Tom smiled. "I say you got a deal."

TWELVE

DANCING WITH THE DAISIES

Karen and her mom scrubbed pots in the sink and loaded up Tom's archaic dishwasher. In spite of all the surprises this morning, Karen couldn't remember a nicer Thanksgiving dinner.

"So, Mom, are you all right?" She dried off a wine glass and put it in the cabinet. "I mean, you know, with…Tom."

"Surprised? Because I am." Bev turned off the water.

"Oh, you could say that." The two of them laughed. "I was worried you and Tom were going to kill each other. Instead, you're…um…"

"Happy?"

Karen got tears in her eyes. "Are you happy?" she asked raggedly.

Bev hugged her. "I am. I know it seems really odd, but Tom and I had a good visit this week. I guess I've been fooling myself for a long time. Your dad and I weren't doing so well. And I needed a good kick in the pants." She pushed back a strand of Karen's hair. "And of course Tom was just the guy to do the kicking."

"I should have done something. I didn't know you were so unhappy. I'm sorry. I—"

"Honey. There was nothing you could do. I raised a smart, happy, healthy child who grew up to be a wonderful young woman. You are my greatest accomplishment. Not the showcase house and garden. I needed to figure out some things on my own. And I guess I just did. At the ripe old age of fifty-nine."

"Mom." Karen's throat clogged up.

"It's okay, honey."

The two of them stood in Tom's kitchen. Embracing, laughing, crying.

"Mom. You know how you've been dreading your sixtieth birthday?"

"Yes."

"Something tells me this is going to be the best year of your life."

Bev smiled. "Something tells me you're right."

"Hey, Dad."

"Yup."

"So you like Mrs. Anderson?" John took a swig of his Bud and set the can on the steps of the porch. He and his dad were hanging on the stoop.

He loved that stoop. He and Karen needed a stoop.

"Yup."

"Hard to believe."

"Yup."

"She doesn't seem like your type."

"Uh-huh."

"She doesn't seem like…um…the casual hookup type either."

Tom narrowed his eyes at John. "Nope, she doesn't. Never thought she was."

John grimaced. Okay, this was getting awkward.

He took a deep breath. "What I mean is, are you seriously interested in her? It sure seems like Bev likes you." Tom said nothing and John plugged on. "I don't want to see Bev get hurt. Not after all those years of shoveling Roger's shit, and um…this is awkward. I'm just wondering—"

"I'm keeping her," Tom finally said with exasperation.

John choked on his beer. "You're keeping her?"

"That's what I said."

"Does she know you're keeping her?"

"Nope. Not yet. Keep it under your hat."

"No problem. Good luck."

"I don't need any goddamned luck. I got daisies."

Beverly and Tom watched the kids pull away in their VW.

Thanksgiving dinner had been nothing like Bev expected. Cranberry sauce from a can. A can! Tom slipped it onto the plate, still intact, with the ridges on the side. He also cooked a surprisingly delicious, moist turkey by inserting a beer can into the cavity of the bird and grilling it.

They ate on paper plates, they drank from plastic cups. There wasn't any good china or crystal or gravy boats. But the day had been fun. And relaxed.

And every time Tom brushed up against her, or squeezed her hand, or whispered something naughty in her ear, happiness bubbled up inside her, fizzing like ginger ale. She felt like a teenager. Giddy. Sexy. Ridiculous. At fifty-nine years old.

In three short days, Tom had sure managed to shake things up. Shake *her* up.

And she didn't mind at all. In spite of this unfamiliar floundering, untethered sensation, she felt lighter and freer than she had in years.

It was simply wonderful.

"Hey, wanna fool around on the sofa? The kids are finally gone." Tom nuzzled her neck.

Bev laughed. "Any chance we could try out your bed this time? Not that I didn't enjoy the couch, but a real bed might be a nice change."

"Beds are for pussies."

"Tom! Language!"

He chuckled. "Look at you. You survived Thanksgiving dinner on a paper plate. I think I won this contest. You didn't think I was serious about the paper plates.

But we did it."

"Oh no." She shook her head. "I won. You had visitors *all day*."

"You ate green apples."

"You mowed the lawn."

"You cut your nails."

"You have flowers in the front of your house."

He bit her earlobe. "You had an orgasm. No, you had multiple orgasms." He pulled back and delivered the smuggest smile possible. "I win."

Bev giggled. "I think I win. I had multiple orgasms." She couldn't deliver the line without blushing, but at least she got the last word.

Tom pinched her bottom.

His expression turned serious. "Do you still feel like you're free-falling without a chute? Or you feeling okay?"

"I'm doing better than okay," she answered softly.

He ran his hands up and down her waist. "You sure look good in my T-shirt."

"I like it. It's comfortable."

"You were just making fun of my clothes a couple of days ago. Now you're wearing them."

She laughed. "You're right. I apologize." She reached up and stroked his stubbly cheek. "I apologize for not being so nice when I got here. I was nervous and worried about the holiday. Worried about being here with you. Alone."

"And now?" He shot her a strange look. Apprehensive. Waiting.

"And now. I like it."

"All of it?" He waggled his brows suggestively.

"All of it." She didn't hesitate with her answer. "I guess I'm a late bloomer."

"I sure like you blooming with me, Bev." The tension drained out of him. "I have an idea."

She leaned against his chest and inhaled his familiar scent. "Uh-oh. What sort of an idea?"

"A damned fine idea. You wanna hear it?" He cleared his throat.

"Sure."

"Say yes first."

"I can't say yes if I don't know—"

"Yes, you can. That way I won't be nervous to ask you." Tom huffed out an impatient breath.

"You really are agitated. Okay, yes. There. Feel better?" *What was this all about?*

He smiled. And pulled out a piece of paper from his back pocket. "Here. This will explain everything."

Beverly read the paper and gasped. It was an itinerary for a British garden tour. And tickets. Two tickets for airfare, the tour, accommodations.

She started to cry.

"No crying. Bev. Come on."

"Tom. This is too much."

"Oh no. No, it's not. It's way past due."

She covered her face with her hands as the tears flowed. He held her gently and whispered in her ear. Whispered nonsense and reassurances.

She gulped and looked up at him. "There are two

tickets here."

"Of course there are. I'm going too."

"You hate prissy gardens."

"Well, I checked with Paul—my nudist neighbor is a travel agent, did I tell you that?—and he said the tour covers history, which I like, and eating at pubs, which I like, and there's beer in England. I like that, too. And some of the tour includes culinary gardens. Practical stuff. And even a garden with poisonous plants. And apple orchards."

"With green and golden apples?" They both laughed.

"All kinds of apples, honey. And daisies." He winked. "So…looks like you're stuck with me."

"Do you even like traveling? You're going to have to…um…talk to people."

"I got us private rooms everywhere. And we have the option to eat on our own or join the group."

"I can't believe you did this. For me." She stared at him in awe. Rough leather-tanned skin, stubbly chin, blue eyes blazing, body hot and hard and safe. "You're making my dream come true."

"Am I? You tell me."

"Just the beginning of it, I think. It's a good place to start."

"Just the beginning."

He kissed her and squeezed her bottom with his big rough hands. "We need to go inside before I give the neighbors a show. Although DiBenedetto probably won't mind. Since he likes giving us a show every goddamned day."

"Tom."

"Hmm." He kissed her neck until she groaned. "That's it. Bedroom. Now."

"Wait." She placed her hand on his chest. "Remember before. When you asked me if I was feeling a little bit fierce?"

He nodded. "Yup. I remember."

"I'm feeling a little bit fierce. Thank you."

He cupped her face and smiled. "That's my girl. Let's go fool around and then we can pack our bags."

Who needed parachutes anyway?

EPILOGUE

CARD FROM CORNWALL

Hello Karen and John!

Tom and I are having a wonderful time in England. We've been gallivanting about the countryside—visiting gardens, exploring castles, and soaking up the history.

Here are some photos from the Lost Gardens of Heligan, including the Edwardian estate and swamp. We toured a fascinating kitchen garden, which Tom adored—lots of vegetables! He has been on a mission to try beer at every pub. So far, he's sampled at least a dozen different kinds (see photo with Tom and barman). He's hoping the Hardin Market will stock some of them when we get home.

We also visited a garden with poisonous plants, and Tom got into a rather heated (and profanity-laced) discussion with our guide. I think she was only mildly traumatized.

Tom wants me to remind you to water the flowers in the front of the house. He said he'll be peeved if he gets home and everything's dead. Also, he wants to know if the gnome has shown up since he left those threatening notices all over the neighborhood.

Last photo! We toured an apple orchard with a remarkable sixteenth century hand-turned cider (spelled cyder!) press. Tom was enamored with the whole thing. They also offered samples of twenty-two varieties of apples. My favorite was the Cornish Honeypin. Wouldn't you know...a golden apple! Tom has been teasing me relentlessly since then. I don't mind so much.

Hope all is well in sunny California. We miss you.

Lots of love,
Bev and Tom

ABOUT THE AUTHOR

PENNY WATSON is a native Pittsburgher whose love of romance started at the age of twelve when she discovered Gone With The Wind in the middle school library. This resulted in numerous attempts at a first novel involving a young lady with windswept hair who lived in a tree house.

A biologist by training, Penny has worked at various times as a dolphin trainer, science teacher, florist, and turfgrass researcher (don't ask). After taking time off to raise her two spirited children, she decided to rekindle her passion for storytelling. Now she gets to incorporate her wide array of interests—including gardening, cooking, and travel—into her works of fiction.

Penny lives outside of Boston with one fly-fishing crazed husband, two lively Filipino kids, and a wiener dog.

To learn more about Penny's upcoming releases visit:

www.pennywatsonbooks.com (website)
www.pennyromance.com (blog)

MORE TITLES BY PENNY WATSON/NINA CLARK

THE KLAUS BROTHERS SERIES

What if the legend of Santa Claus is real? What if Santa has five strapping sons who help him run his empire? Five single, sexy sons looking for romance?

SWEET INSPIRATION
Klaus Brothers Series #1

Nicholas Klaus is a master pastry chef, a strict disciplinarian, and the eldest son of the legendary Santa Claus. One look at café owner Lucy Brewster sends him into an unexpected tailspin of lusty desires. When Lucy is injured, Nicholas makes a decision that catapults both of their lives into turmoil...

Lucy Brewster, the free-spirited proprietor of Sweet Inspiration, has a flair for concocting sugary confections but no time for adventure. She gets more than she bargained for when she awakens in the North Pole... rambunctious elves, a fitness-obsessed Santa, and the man of her dreams.

Does she have what it takes to become the next Mrs. Klaus?

SWEET MAGIK
KLAUS BROTHERS SERIES #2

Oskar Klaus' job is killing him. Not even his favorite hobbies (extreme snowboarding and browsing old bookstores) are enough to snap him out of his funk. It's not easy living in the shadow of four successful older brothers and a father named Santa. Little does he know that a kiss on New Year's Eve is about to turn his life upside-down.

Kiana Grant's Manhattan life is a world away from her childhood in Oahu. She traded sunsets and surfing for a respectable career in library science, but Oskar Klaus is a temptation that's hard to resist. Before she knows it, she's in the midst of an outrageous adventure in the North Pole, dealing with mischievous elves, wicked demons, and a devastating attraction to Santa's youngest son.

There's just one problem...a bitter elf hell-bent on revenge threatens the future of everyone in the North Pole, even Santa himself...

LUMBERJACK IN LOVE

"The delicious beard! The magnificent log!
This city-girl-meets-lumberjack tale
is a crazy sexy hairy delight."
— Carolyn Crane, author of The Disillusionists Trilogy

City slicker Ami Jordan was just dumped by her back-stabbing boyfriend, has no job prospects, and can't find a decent cup of coffee in the entire state of Vermont. The last thing she needs is a sexy, bearded lumberjack complicating her life. Even if he's smart, talented, and has the hottest ass she's ever seen.

Tree house builder, environmental champion, and Bulldog owner Marcus Anderson has no patience for flatlanders with an attitude. But when landscape designer Ami Jordan shows up at his log cabin, he suddenly develops a hankering for a high-maintenance city gal. Now his house looks like a jungle, his recycling is in disarray, and his libido's on fire.

He's a lumberjack in love.

Check out the new children's series by
Nina Clark and Sara Pulver:

LUCY THE WONDER WEENIE!

Lucy the Diva Doxie irritates her family with an obsessive licking habit. Then one day she consumes a pile of magic beans and something extraordinary happens. She transforms into LUCY THE WONDER WEENIE. After adopting her new super hero persona, Lucy makes a startling discovery. Her bothersome habit has the power to comfort tearful children and create laughter, love, and joy.

Because every dog's a superhero.

72349227R00073

Made in the USA
Middletown, DE
04 May 2018